PHANTOM RAIDER

The rustler's eyes widened when he looked up and saw Slocum in the saddle and didn't recognize him as one of his partners. Slocum was already going for his Colt Navy but froze and just stared when he got the drop on the man.

"Mayes!" cried Slocum. He settled back in the saddle, let down the hammer on his six-gun, and lifted the muzzle to point skyward. The rustler took the opportunity to dodge into the pitch-black night and vanish like a ghost. Seconds later came the pounding of a solitary horse's hooves. The rustler had escaped. And Slocum had let him go when he had the drop on him.

"Joel Mayes," he said in disbelief. "I saw them shoot you in the back. You're dead."

DON'T MISS THESE
ALL-ACTION WESTERN SERIES
FROM THE BERKLEY PUBLISHING GROUP

THE GUNSMITH by J. R. Roberts
Clint Adams was a legend among lawmen, outlaws, and ladies. They called him . . . the Gunsmith.

LONGARM by Tabor Evans
The popular long-running series about U.S. Deputy Marshal Long—his life, his loves, his fight for justice.

LONE STAR by Wesley Ellis
The blazing adventures of Jessica Starbuck and the martial arts master, Ki. Over eight million copies in print.

SLOCUM by Jake Logan
Today's longest-running action Western. John Slocum rides a deadly trail of hot blood and cold steel.

JAKE LOGAN

SLOCUM AND QUANTRILL

BERKLEY BOOKS, NEW YORK

SLOCUM AND QUANTRILL

A Berkley Book / published by arrangement with
the author

PRINTING HISTORY
Berkley edition / October 1994

ISBN: 0-425-14400-3

BERKLEY®
Berkley Books are published by The Berkley Publishing Group,
200 Madison Avenue, New York, New York, 10016.
BERKLEY and the "B" design
are trademarks belonging to Berkley Publishing Corporation.

PRINTED IN THE UNITED STATES OF AMERICA

10 9 8 7 6 5 4 3 2 1

1

John Slocum missed death by an inch as the steer horn ripped through his shirt. He slammed backward into the fence and tried to slip past the angry, fighting steer.

"You look out now, Slocum. That there walkin' Delmonico steak ain't happy with you," laughed another cowboy. Davey Lee Watkins made no move to keep the steer moving along the chute toward the feed pens. "It knows what you're gonna do to it."

"Help me, dammit," Slocum called. The steer side-stepped and leaned against him, pinning him. If he dropped, the steer would hook him again. The horn tips had been polled before the drive began from down in Texas, but that didn't make the animal any less dangerous. The rounded hunk of horn was backed with twelve hundred pounds of pure mean and muscle. The Shawnee Trail hadn't been too kind to either drover or animal, drought taking its toll. The beeves were spooked easily, and arriving in Kansas City hadn't helped their disposition one little bit.

"You're doin' just fine," Davey Lee said, enjoying Slocum's problem. Slocum would have bashed in the young cowboy's face if he could have gotten out of his predicament. The air was being crushed from his lungs as the steer continued leaning against him.

Slocum slammed his elbows against the steer's back, but the animal wouldn't budge. He kicked and got his boot heel on the lowest slat in the chute. Pushing hard, Slocum slipped up and over the back of the steer. The steer saw it had no chance to gore or crush him now, so it changed tactics with cunning only a trapped brute could muster. It began bucking, trying to toss Slocum over its head to the ground in front, where it could get at him again.

Slocum grabbed a horn and was flung to and fro like a child's rag doll. The battering against the chute walls rattled his teeth, but Slocum knew he would be dead if he fell. The pawing hooves, the tossing horns, the hard-kicking back legs—any of them would crush his skull like an eggshell.

"Ride 'em, Slocum!" shouted Davey Lee Watkins. "You got 'im scared now. Keep on top!"

Other cowboys from the drive gathered to watch. Slocum cursed steadily as he fought to stay on the steer long enough to get it out of the chute. When the steer burst into the corral, Slocum kicked free. He hit the ground running and lost his footing in the muck. It took a few seconds for the steer to stop its frantic run.

It turned, pawed the ground, and looked for him. Slocum got to his feet and stood stock-still. He knew the steer couldn't see him if he stayed squarely in front of it. The animal snorted a bit, then stupidly forgot what had angered it. Turning, the steer went to explore the feed pen. Only then did Slocum back off until he hit the corral fence. He scrambled up and over, landing heavily outside.

"You done real good, Slocum. I always said you was the best of us." Davey Lee laughed heartily. He wasn't laughing so hard when Slocum reared back and unloaded a haymaker that sent the cowboy staggering. Davey Lee sat down heavily, his eyes glazed by the force of the blow.

"I could have been killed," Slocum said coldly. "We're supposed to help each other."

Others he had ridden with came to Davey Lee Watkins's aid, moving to face down Slocum. It had been like this all the way north. Slocum had never much liked any of the men, and the dislike had grown to outright hostility with every mile along the trail. But Slocum needed the job, and the Double Ought ranch's owner, Charles Jefferson, paid top dollar.

"You're going too far, Slocum," said one of the men Slocum considered a stone killer. Healey's hand twitched at his side as he got ready to draw. Slocum knew he might have to throw down on Healey, and he knew who would be dead. Slocum's rage faded and a cold calm filled him. His green eyes stared into Healey's bloodshot brown ones, looking for any hint of motion.

The first muscle twitch in Healey's shoulders would send Slocum going for the Colt Navy in his cross-draw holster.

"Hey, Slocum, Potter wants to see you," came the shout from the far side of the feedlot. "Right now."

"What's it going to be, Healey?" Slocum asked. "It'll only take a second for you to die."

Healey's hand twitched a bit more, but the telltale movements of a man going for his six-shooter weren't there. Slocum saw a tic working under Healey's eye, and the man started looking left and right, for support among the others. It wasn't there. They knew who would die if the shooting started.

"You'd better get on over to the foreman's shack," another cowboy said. "You know how Potter gets when we don't jump when he says 'frog.' "

"I know how he gets when one of his men ends up dead, too," Slocum said. "Might as well tell him I was late because I was busy putting a slug in a worthless cayuse's belly."

"Go on, Slocum. We kin settle this later. Jist you and me," Healey said. Slocum knew the only way Healey was likely to conclude this was a bullet to his back. If Charles Jefferson hadn't paid so well, Slocum would have been on his way a long time back. This pointless dispute with Watkins and Healey only hurried his desire to find new horizons.

When Healey stepped back and turned away, Slocum knew he was safe enough for the moment. Slocum snorted in disgust, stared after Healey and Watkins, then spat in the direction of the steer pawing and charging around the feed pen. For two cents, Slocum would have taken a rifle and turned the steer into a good dinner.

He made his way through the stockyard, thinking it might be time for him to claim his pay and clear out. Jefferson had told them they had to stay on until the middle of the month, but Slocum figured he could talk the cattle owner out of his pay now. First he'd see what Horn Potter had to say.

Slocum and the foreman hadn't got on too well, either, so he wasn't eager to see the short, stumpy man with the drooping walrus-style mustache. Potter had been too strident and demanding for Slocum's taste, even when there was no call to shout and carry on.

"About time you got your worthless butt here, Slocum," snapped Potter. The man boiled out from a small shack where the Double Ought foreman had an office. Potter shoved Slocum hard to keep him from entering, then backed off when he saw the tombstones in Slocum's eyes. Slocum had been pushed around too much to take any ill use from the likes of the foreman.

"What do you want?" Slocum crossed his arms and glared at the foreman.

"Some longhorns got out of their pen. Go track 'em down and bring 'em back." The foreman thrust out his chin belligerently and crossed his arms, matching Slocum's stance. "Earn your pay, for a change."

Slocum knew he was the best hand on the Double Ought drive—and he knew both Jefferson and his foreman knew it. But Potter wasn't going to back down. To do so would diminish his stature in his own mind and in the eyes of the other cowboys.

"Why not pay me off and let Healey go fetch the beeves?" suggested Slocum. "It's about time for me to move on."

"I want *you* to round up those beeves." Potter puffed himself up even more, and Slocum saw that this had turned into a power battle. Nothing short of finding the lost cattle would save Potter's reputation for being a tough boss. Slocum considered simply walking away, but he needed the pay. He wasn't about to forfeit three months' wages, not when he had put up with bad food, terrible weather, and other drovers who had gone out of their way to make life miserable for him. Slocum was more than owed the money. He deserved it.

"I'll find the critters, *then* you can pay me what's owed."

"Mr. Jefferson wants everybody on the payroll till the fifteenth. If you up and leave with your pay right now, the others will want theirs, too. And that ain't gonna happen."

This wasn't Slocum's problem. He couldn't care less what the other drovers wanted or why Jefferson wanted to keep his full complement of range hands until midmonth. Staying another twelve days wasn't in the cards for Slocum.

"We'll talk this over when I get back," he said. "How many beeves are missing?"

"A few dozen head," came the startling answer. Sales on that many cattle would more than pay Slocum's salary for the summer.

"Which pen?"

Potter pointed, and Slocum walked away without asking any more. A few dozen beeves didn't simply run off.

Somebody had to help them. When Slocum got to the feed pen, he saw that his guess was right. The leather thong holding the gate shut had been cut cleanly with a sharp knife. If the cattle had managed to bang up against the gate, there'd have been frayed ends and other evidence of bovine destruction.

Heaving a sigh, considering this was more the sheriff's province than his own, Slocum fetched his gear. He had the notion he'd be on the trail of those cattle for a good long time before finding them—if he ever did.

It was nearing twilight when Slocum came back into Kansas City herding fourteen of the lost beeves. He considered himself lucky in finding them so quickly. From the condition of the trail he could only guess what had happened. The hooves had cut up the grass and turned muddy spots into a real swamp, but he saw occasional shod hoofprints paralleling the trail taken by the cattle, proving that they had been rustled. This small herd had broken away from the others and had gone down near a small creek for water. The rustlers either didn't want to go chasing the stolen Double Ought cattle, or they were spooked and thought the law might be on their trail.

They had all the time in the world, if they had only known. Slocum could never have fought the number of men it had taken to get a sizeable herd moving. More to the point he wouldn't have bothered. Getting himself killed over any part of Charles Jefferson's herd wasn't in the cards for him. He felt no allegiance to the rancher and even less to his foreman.

Slocum had worked for some outfits where he would have died for the owner and any of the hands riding beside him on the trail. But not for the Double Ought crew.

"Get on in there. You're due to be steaks before long," Slocum called to keep the cattle moving. He applied the end of his lariat to a few bovine rumps and then roped shut their pen. Slocum dropped from the saddle, weary and more than a little angry at the foreman for not sending anyone to help him.

"What the hell are you doin' here, Slocum?" came an angry voice Slocum recognized as Charles Jefferson's.

"Got a few of the cattle back," Slocum said. "Looks as if they were rustled. I found the gate pen—"

"Get back there and find the rest. Potter told me how you were malingering." The rancher looked fit to be tied. Slocum had seen him mad before, but not like this. His ordinarily florid face was flushed, and he snorted and pawed around like a bull with a red flag flapping in front of it.

"I don't understand. Malingering?"

"You weren't doing your damned job!" roared Jefferson. "Get your ass back out there and find the steers that wandered off."

"You weren't listening to what I said, Mr. Jefferson," Slocum said softly, wondering why he was even bothering. Then he touched his shirt pocket and knew. He wanted his money. For three months he had eaten rotten food and spent long hours in the saddle getting these beeves to Kansas City. He was owed the money, and he would collect it. "They were stolen, taken from the pens. If you want the rest back, track them down yourself—and I'd suggest you take the sheriff with you."

Jefferson cooled down a mite, but the anger still flashed in his pale eyes. "You want your pay? You go fetch back those cows."

Slocum hesitated. He knew he could take the money from Jefferson. The man was paunchy and didn't have the reflexes to use the hogleg swinging at his side, but that wouldn't be right if he could get his pay in a proper fashion.

"A reward for bringing them back?" he suggested. This set Jefferson off again.

"You damned thief! Not one red cent until you get those cattle into my feed pens. I swear, I'll see you in jail, too. I'll string you up!"

Slocum didn't know what the cattleman's problem was, but he didn't appreciate the situation. His fingers tapped lightly against his gunbelt as he wondered if Jefferson carried the equivalent of a summer's pay on him. The rancher stiffened as if he could read Slocum's thoughts.

"Horn! Horn!" he bellowed. From across the corral rushed the foreman.

"You try tellin' Slocum to do his job. I ain't payin' him anything till he brings back those missing cattle." Charles Jefferson swung about and stormed off, leaving Slocum to wonder what the trouble really was. The missing beeves weren't his responsibility. Something else worried Jefferson like a burr under his saddle blanket.

"You heard him, Slocum. Get into the saddle and find them. They couldn't have wandered too far, now, could they?"

"They were stolen, and you know it. Get some of the others to come with me and I'll get the rustlers. There might even be a reward for such bold cattle thieves," Slocum said.

"You been told what to do. Go do it," Horn Potter snapped. He turned and followed his boss.

Slocum saw he wasn't going to get paid unless he found the other cattle and returned them. He didn't know exactly how many were still missing. Maybe two dozen, maybe more. The thought crossed his mind that there was no reason to come back if he found the cattle. Ten would pay him real well for the time and trouble with the Double Ought outfit. Slocum wasn't keen on turning any man in for rustling, but that might be a few dollars extra for his trouble.

Watering and feeding his gray gelding, Slocum took a few minutes to eat himself. Only then did he head back into the gathering gloom of night. He had a good idea of the direction taken by the rustlers. He traveled light and fast. With any luck he thought he could overtake them before midnight—if they kept moving in a beeline away from Kansas City.

Wobbling in the saddle from lack of sleep, Slocum kept moving along doggedly and almost ran over the rustlers' camp. He topped a rise and saw a dried cow-chip fire burning with sullen intensity. The three men seated around it all jumped to their feet, hands going to their six-shooters.

"It's the law," cried one. "They musta got Joel, or he'd've warned us!" The other two lit out running for their horses. Slocum was jolted away when one took a shot at him. In the dark there was little chance of hitting him, but it spooked his horse. Slocum had to fight for a moment to keep the spirited animal under control. By the time he got his seat back, the three rustlers had hightailed it into the night.

Slocum rode down into their camp slowly, thinking that they were mighty skittish for seasoned cattle thieves. He heard the mournful lowing of the beeves and knew he had a real chore ahead of him. He had recovered more than thirty head.

He couldn't decide if he wanted to try moving the sleepy cattle to put as much distance as he could between him and the rustlers or if he could grab a few hours' sleep. He decided to move on right away. The rustlers might take it into their heads to return and find there wasn't an entire posse backing up the solitary rider they'd spotted.

"Let's get a-moving," Slocum called out, and he rode around the small knot of cattle. But as he worked, a small detail niggled away at the back of his mind. The rustlers had thought their sentry had been taken out, but Slocum hadn't seen a lookout. Almost at the same instant, Slocum rode up on a man on the ground. He had worried himself a small depression under a sage and was sleeping, thinking there wasn't any need for a watch out on the prairie.

"What's goin' on?" came the sleepy voice. "You out there molestin' those cows again, you horny old goat?"

The rustler's eyes widened when he looked up and saw Slocum in the saddle and didn't recognize him as one of his partners. Slocum was already going for his Colt Navy but froze and just stared when he got the drop on the man.

"Mayes!" cried Slocum. He settled back in the saddle, let down the hammer on his six-gun, and lifted the muzzle to point skyward. The rustler took the opportunity to dodge into the pitch-black night and vanish like a ghost. Seconds later came the pounding of a solitary horse's hooves. The rustler had escaped. And Slocum had let him go when he had the drop on him.

"Joel Mayes," he said in disbelief. "I saw them shoot you in the back. You're dead."

2

September 4, 1882

"I saw you killed," Slocum muttered. He realized he still clung to his Colt Navy. He slowly slipped it back into his holster, wondering who he had really seen. Maybe hearing one rustler call the name "Joel" had set off a string of buried memories. It had been a while since Slocum had been in Kansas City—and that was where he'd ridden with Joel Mayes back in 1863.

He had been another of Quantrill's Raiders, one of the worst. Yet Slocum had gotten along with the guerrilla sergeant good enough. Not so's to be friends, but good enough. Slocum had seen Mayes take a bullet in the back as they rode from a town they had just pistoled. Slocum couldn't even remember the name of the town or why they had filled the buildings with hundreds of slugs. There had been too many raids like that one, and the only thing making this memorable was its occurrence a week before the Lawrence, Kansas, raid.

There had been too many civilians killed—and too many of the ruthless men riding with Quantrill, too.

Slocum rubbed his belly, tracing out the scars where he had been gut-shot by Bloody Bill Anderson for protesting the Lawrence massacre. Quantrill had ridden into that town to protest personal loss, ordering every man and boy slaughtered. Among other murders, Slocum had seen an eight-year-old boy gunned down when he

11

couldn't find shelter quick enough. That had rankled. Slocum had his own ideas of how to wage war, and killing children didn't enter into it.

Bill Anderson had laughed when he shot Slocum three times, shouting that there was no place in Quantrill's Raiders for a yellow-belly.

Slocum hadn't been the first shot riding with Quantrill, and he had heard he wasn't the last. But he had seen Joel Mayes fall from the saddle a week earlier. No man could have lived after being injured like that. The bullet must have shattered his spine.

"A ghost," muttered Slocum. He snorted in disgust as he shook his head. He didn't abide by ghosts or other supernatural things people seemed so fond of citing as authorities for all things. "More likely just somebody who looks a powerful lot like Mayes." It had been almost twenty years, and he had aged. Mayes would have, too, and Slocum knew he was just guessing what Mayes would look like now.

He wheeled his gray around and began the tedious job of driving the herd of cattle back toward Kansas City. Slocum had been dog tired before finding the rustlers, and now he was having a hard time keeping his eyes open. He fumbled out his brother Robert's watch and snapped open the cover. Peering at the dial in the faint starlight, he saw it was almost one o'clock.

Slocum heaved a sigh and put the spurs to his horse's flanks. The gray gelding jumped and cut across the front of the herd, turning the direction enough to get them back on what passed for a road in these parts. Wishing he had another cowboy with him to keep the dawdling steers in the herd, Slocum moved in a continuous arc back and forth behind the herd until he sighted the city lights.

He counted twenty-two head of cattle, more than enough to pay him for the three months on the trail and the trouble of wresting the beeves from rustlers.

But if he took the cattle, he'd be a rustler, too. That part didn't worry Slocum too much. He had done worse in his day.

His mind wandered back to his days with Quantrill's Raiders. And Joel Mayes. The man had a scar under his left eye. He tried to remember if the rustler he saw earlier had had such a scar. Slocum had a good memory for such things, but he wasn't sure. There might have been a brighter pink scar marring the man's leathery face, or it might have been a trick of light. There wasn't anything more than stars out tonight, the Milky Way giving an eerie aspect to everything and everyone.

"No scar," Slocum said, trying to convince himself. "I didn't see a scar." But he wasn't sure. The rustler's face had been smudged with dirt. That might have hidden a scar. Slocum yelled in anger at the cattle, to vent his own frustration. He was talking himself into believing he'd seen a dead man. Mayes had been shot in the back, and that was the end of a sorry life.

Somehow, as Slocum argued with himself, he kept the herd moving toward Kansas City. Realizing now that he had decided to stick around with the Double Ought crew until mid-month, Slocum resigned himself to getting only his pay. There wouldn't be any bonus for bringing in the stolen beeves. If anything, he could expect another cussing out for being so slow. He didn't understand Charles Jefferson, but Slocum didn't especially want to try.

All he wanted was his due.

Slocum got the steers into a pen and made sure it was secured. He looked around for Horn Potter and found his shack empty. The foreman might be out whooping and hollering with the rest of the cowboys. Kansas City was a wide-open town, and the saloons ran twenty-four hours a day. Slocum didn't know where to find Jefferson to report his success, so he decided to spend the few dollars riding in his pocket on a bottle of whiskey.

He had earned it with the extra duty. Slocum tended his gelding and then started for the main street running through the belly of Kansas City. Gaslights flared on either side of the street and the sounds of boisterous laughter echoed from any number of the dance halls and casinos. Slocum touched his shirt pocket and felt the two-and-a-half-dollar gold piece riding there and knew a poker game was out of the question. He needed his entire pay from the Double Ought drive to get into a serious game.

But he had enough money for whiskey. He ignored the busier saloons in favor of a quieter place. He had to sit and think through everything he had seen tonight.

"What'll it be?" called a friendly barkeep as Slocum strode in to a ramshackle bar. "You look dusty and just off the trail. Try this. Specialty of the house." The barkeep poured a pale amber concoction into a shot glass. Slocum hesitated until the bartender said, "Go on, go on. It's on the house. First one for you fellows always is."

Slocum sampled the drink. It had the kick of a full-grown mule. It sizzled and burned all the way down his throat and puddled hotly in his belly.

"Really something, ain't it? My own special recipe. Secret, it is, but it'll get you drunker than a skunk. Another?"

"It's chewing its way through my stomach," Slocum complained. He knew many of the barkeeps laced their liquor with nitric acid to improve the punch. Slocum preferred something more sedate, even trade whiskey boiled together with gunpowder and rusty nails for color and body.

"Two or three more and you won't care."

"A bottle of rye," Slocum ordered. "That's one powerful drink, but not for me. Not tonight."

"Here's your bottle," the barkeep said. Slocum saw that it lacked several fingers of being a full bottle, but he still paid the entire price. That was the way it was done in the cow towns. If being shorted a drink or two was the only way he was being cheated, Slocum would feel he had come out ahead.

"Might I interest you in something to go with that fine whiskey?" The barkeep tipped his head in the direction of a rear door. "There's some mighty fine-lookin' ladies out back waitin' for a stallion like you. Reasonable prices, too." The barkeep saw Slocum's lack of interest. "For a cowboy just off the trail, there's a first-time price of two bits. Can't match the price or the product anywhere else in Kansas City."

"I'm sure," Slocum said. "Maybe later." He knew walking out that back door might get him laid. It might also get him killed. More than one saloon hired thugs to waylay horny drovers as they drunkenly stumbled out to the cribs in search of a whore.

Slocum wasn't in a mood to kill anyone right now, not for trying to rob him. If Horn Potter or even Charles Jefferson walked up and started badgering him, that was another matter.

Taking his bottle to a far table, Slocum settled down and stared across the room. Only a few patrons drank, mostly in silence like him. Turning halfway let Slocum look out a window into the main street. He caught his own partial reflection in the window. For a moment, he just stared, then he reached up and touched the spot under his left eye.

"That rustler *did* have a scar, just like Mayes," Slocum said. He shuddered. It was uncanny how one man might look like another dead these nineteen years. He had listened to the cowboys sitting around camp fires late at night telling tall tales of how they'd run into men who looked exactly like them or their dead brothers or whoever. Slocum had always taken such stories with a grain of salt. There wasn't anybody out there who looked and acted like him, and there certainly wasn't another

Joel Mayes rustling cattle in Kansas.

Slocum took a long drink and started to refill his glass. A long shadow fell across his table. He glanced up, expecting to see the Double Ought foreman. Instead, a slender man, hardly five-foot-nine, stood with his feet far apart and his hand resting on the butt of a six-gun swinging at his hip. A bright seven-pointed star shone on his chest. Slocum had seen others like it beaten out of silver Mexican pesos. Those wearing such gaudy symbols of their office were usually more bothersome than effective.

"You Slocum?"

"Reckon so, Sheriff," Slocum said, leaning back. He kept his hands on the table. He saw the muscles twitching in the lawman's shoulders, indicating he wanted to draw down on Slocum. "What can I do for you? A drink?"

"Don't go sassin' me, boy," snapped the sheriff. "You bring in those cattle belonging to Charles Jefferson?"

"The foremen and Mr. Jefferson sent me out to find the cattle. I did, and when I got back, I put them in their corral for fattening."

"So?" The lawman was turning more belligerent.

"I don't rightly understand you, Sheriff. What are you asking me?" Slocum placed his hands flat on the table. In this position he might get to his Colt before the sheriff started his draw. Slocum was fast but didn't know how fast this quivering lawman might be. Whatever happened, Slocum wasn't going to go to jail.

He had led a life filled with bullet and gunsmoke, doing his share of killing. He didn't know if the sheriff had seen one of a dozen wanted posters circulating through the West, but he wasn't going to simply sit and palaver. That wasn't his way.

"Where'd you find that many cows?"

"East of town," Slocum said. "You seem to be accusing me of something, Sheriff. Spit it out."

"You found them cows too easy," the sheriff said. "I'm wondering if you rustled them yourself."

"Be mighty stupid of me to steal the cows, get clean away with it, then have the foreman send me out to fetch beeves I'd already stolen, then bring them all back."

"You got a mouth on you, Slocum. I don't like men who—"

"Sheriff, I found the cattle like I was told. I brought them back. Is Mr. Jefferson filing charges against me for cattle rustling?"

"No, but—"

"Is the foreman? Horn Potter doesn't have the sense God gave a goose. They told me to do my job, and I did. There's nothing wrong in that."

"What about the rustlers? What did they look like?" demanded the sheriff. Slocum was getting tired of the man's attitude. He knew the sheriff couldn't stand all primed to draw forever. His muscle twitching was getting worse. He'd either have to draw or back down. Slocum knew which way he was going to bet.

"Didn't see any rustlers," Slocum lied. "I found the herd drinking at a stock tank. Can't imagine how anyone could have left the corral gate open like that, but Horn Potter's not too good a foreman. He might have done it, or one of the other Double Ought hands."

"You sayin' the foreman's responsible?"

Slocum shook his head and held up his glass with his left hand in a silent salute to the lawman. He knew he had won. The sheriff settled back on his heels, and his hand moved from the butt of his six-shooter to loop a thumb through his gunbelt.

"We don't like your kind in Kansas City, Slocum. I'd highly suggest that you ride on out as fast as your horse will take you." The sheriff spun around and stormed out, his heels clicking loudly on the sagging saloon floor.

Slocum heaved a sigh of relief when the swinging doors closed behind the lawman. He didn't know what had put the bug in the sheriff's ear, but it had been a powerful one. He was less and less inclined to stay in Kansas City and more intent on finding Charles Jefferson to demand his money. The sheriff might not suspect him of actually rustling the cattle, but the man's mind was turning in that direction.

Getting away from a man intending to jail him struck Slocum as a wise course. He knocked back another glass of the whiskey and almost wished he had bought the barkeep's special blend. He needed something more than the tarantula juice he was swilling. But enough, even of this weak sister to the nitric acid–laced beverage, would suffice.

When the bottle was less than half-full, Slocum slowed his steady drinking. His mind kept wandering from the Double Ought cattle to Horn Potter and Jefferson— and to Joel Mayes. He tried to force from his mind the image of Mayes tumbling from his horse, a bright red splotch spreading like wildfire on the back of his butternut-colored guerrilla shirt. The harder he tried, the more persistent the memory became.

"The rustler had a scar, just like Mayes," Slocum declared aloud. The barkeep looked quizzically in his direction, then went back to talking with a gambler at the bar. Settling back in his chair, resting only the back two legs on the floor, Slocum stared into the street again. He had a better view of the alley running alongside the saloon, and in it he saw two men whispering.

When a young woman hurried along the boardwalk and stepped into the mouth of the alley, the two hoodlums acted. They rushed from the alley and pulled her into the darkness.

Slocum was already out of his chair and heading for the rear door. The barkeep called to him, asking which of the women in the cribs he might want. Slocum ignored him as he slipped his six-gun from its holster. He spun around the side of the saloon into the alley and saw one man forcing the young woman against the saloon wall. The other stood back a pace, a long, wicked knife in his hand.

Slocum never hesitated. He covered the distance between them in a flash. He swung his six-shooter and smashed the barrel into the knife-wielding man's head. The man went down in a boneless pile, never uttering a single word. The woman's eyes widened when she saw what had happened, but she didn't cry out.

Slocum took one step forward and cocked his Colt. He placed the cold muzzle against the second hoodlum's neck.

"Let her go," he said in a cold voice. "I buffaloed your partner. I might just blow your head off, if the mood strikes me right."

"You got this wrong, mister," the would-be robber protested. "Me and the lady was talking over a business deal."

Slocum eyed the young woman curiously. No fear marked her lovely face. She had cornflower-blue eyes, a long, thin nose, and fair, reddish hair. Her full lips pulled back in a half smile, as if mocking him for his gallantry. But there was something more than caused Slocum to lose his concentration.

He recognized her. And yet he didn't.

This moment of inattention let the hoodlum duck under the gun and shove Slocum backward. Slocum was enough off balance that he didn't chance a shot for fear of hitting the woman. And then the robber was gone into the night.

"Thank you, John," she said.

"You know me?" Slocum was more puzzled than ever. He couldn't quite place her, and yet he would never forget any woman this beautiful. Her blue eyes fixed boldly on him. He could only describe her as haunting.

"You are John Slocum, aren't you?"

"Yes, but I don't remember you. I'm sorry about that."
He was more confused than ever. He slid his six-shooter
back into his cross-draw holster and touched the brim of
his hat.

"Such a gentleman, but then you would be, coming
from Georgia. The most chivalrous and bold men come
from the South, don't you agree?" She seemed to be
teasing him.

"Reckon so, if you say it," Slocum allowed. He fought
to remember her name, a first name, a last. He couldn't
remember ever meeting her.

She laughed deliciously at his obvious confusion and
reached out to touch his cheek. Slocum wasn't sure how
to react.

"A proper young lady wouldn't be so bold, would she?
But then my father wasn't a Southern gentleman."

"Your father?"

"He came from Ohio."

Slocum felt as if the ground had opened up and he
had begun tumbling endlessly through empty space.

"You knew him well, didn't you, John? He was
William Quantrill. And I'm his daughter, Laura. Laura
Quantrill."

3

General Tom Hindman stood behind his desk at his Little Rock headquarters, hands clasped behind him and smiling ear to ear. Captain John Slocum stood at attention, waiting for his general to finish giving him his orders. Captain Slocum wasn't sure he cottoned much to the Confederate Partisan Ranger Act, but war beyond the Mississippi was different from back East.

"I received the orders July 17 from the War Department," Hindman said, not doing too good a job holding back his glee. "I'd already drafted my own guerrilla act, but this is better. It is. It might turn the war in the Trans-Mississippi Region for us, Captain." Hindman began pacing and his mood turned grim. Slocum's knees were beginning to hurt from standing at attention this long. He was more used to hiking along with the troops moving through Arkansas, usually in retreat. Pea Ridge had been a major defeat.

"President Davis doesn't believe in guerrilla warfare, but the Congress gave us the Partisan Ranger Act." Hindman looked up and saw Slocum was more concerned with not falling over than with listening. "Sorry, Captain. Sit down. I forget you've been a-march for the last week."

"Thank you, sir." Slocum gratefully sank into the straight-backed chair by the general's desk. "My boots have holes in the soles, and the blisters were starting to hurt again."

Hindman shook his head. "Damn Jeff Davis," he muttered under his breath. Slocum said nothing. He shared his general's concern for the way President Davis insisted on intruding in day-to-day operation of the army. For all the true concern, Slocum considered many of Davis's orders crippling and responsible for much of the Confederacy's defeats. Better to let the able generals from Lee on down plot the strategy.

"We'll see about getting you a horse, even if I have to lend you my personal steed." Hindman began pacing again. "This mission is of utmost importance to the South, Captain. I have authorized Quantrill to form a unit to harass Schofield and Halleck, especially Halleck, damn his eyes!"

"I've heard rumors the Federals have issued orders to shoot any guerrilla on sight," Slocum ventured. From the rumors he had heard about William Clark Quantrill, there was some reason. Quantrill burned and killed at will, aiming as much at civilians as he did at military targets.

"Their General Order Eighteen," Hindman supplied. "Extermination, complete and total. They've been burning out entire towns and exiled the residents simply because they think there might be Southern sympathizers in the populace." Hindman dropped into the chair behind his desk and stared squarely into Slocum's unflinching green eyes. "This can help us, Captain. Halleck is creating support for our cause by his actions. Some of the guerrillas might have family in those towns, but mostly the Federals are using this as an excuse to seize property they need for their troops."

"I've heard tell Quantrill does much the same."

"That's why I need you to relay my orders to him," Hindman said. He leaned forward and his expression turned stern. "You're about the best officer I have on my staff, Captain. I need you to oversee Quantrill and keep him in check."

"How am I supposed to do that, unless I'm in charge of his soldiers?" asked Slocum. He disliked being a courier almost as much as he did being set to play nursemaid to another officer. "I'd prefer remaining with your staff, General."

"You can be of inestimable service to the Confederacy in Missouri, Captain. I need eyes and ears there. I need reliable reports. Without that, we might lose the entire Trans-Mississippi region. You know the importance of Missouri and everything to the west."

"Yes, sir, I do," said Slocum. "I don't rightly know how I can operate as you want, unless I'm in charge. If I'm assigned to his unit and under Quantrill's orders, I might have a time of nosing around for you." Slocum danced around saying what he really meant. A guerrilla band moved fast, and maintaining reliable lines of communication back to General Hindman would be well-nigh impossible. If Slocum tried, Quantrill might take it into his head to simply execute him as a spy. In the field, who was to say how a captain died, especially if the reports were less than favorable?

"You're resourceful, Slocum. I've watched you. There's no better marksman in my command, and you can ride with the best of our cavalry. Jackson would have loved having you at his right hand." Hindman leaned forward even more and lowered his voice, talking in a conspiratorial whisper to keep Slocum's attention.

"Quantrill is a wild card out in the field, Captain. I need a trump to use, if it comes to that. You are that trump."

"I always do my best, sir," Slocum said, knowing he was being ordered on the very mission he hated most. "Have you the orders for Quantrill?"

"Not so fast. I want you to carry his commission. He, too, is to be a captain."

Slocum held back the groan that threatened to come out. Having two officers the same rank in a unit spelled disaster, if one was legally in charge. Better to make Quantrill a brevet major than let both of them ride with captain's bars. The one with the faster gun would be the only one left in command.

"My future campaigns require heavy recruiting in Missouri. I need you to send me recruits, wherever you find them. I can handle the supply problems. Jeff Davis has to be convinced that the war in Arkansas and Missouri is as important as that in Virginia and Tennessee."

"I've heard of the roundups of deserters," Slocum said. "How good a unit can you put together with men wanting to be elsewhere?"

"Not your concern, Captain," Hindman said briskly. He waved his hand in the air, as if erasing the comment. "General Porter needs support if we are to invade Missouri in strength and flank the Federal forces along the Mississippi. This is the basis for ordering partisan bands to operate."

Hindman shot to his feet and came around the desk. He fished inside his gray wool uniform jacket and drew forth a sheaf of papers. He thrust them out for Slocum.

"These are Quantrill's orders, with his commission as captain. You can scan the orders."

Slocum glanced over the long lines of printed material. How ten men could form a band, with a captain, sergeant, and corporal. But the part that would send shivers of fear into the Federals came a few lines later. The captain was free to act without orders from higher up in the chain of command. Any gunboats or transports, Federal pickets, scouts, foraging parties, or trains were fair game. The orders specifically called for the immediate executions of train engineers and boat pilots.

Slocum knew Quantrill would never get to the third part of the orders, stating that the partisans were under the same regulations as regular troops.

"I've authorized Colonels Hays, Hughes, Cockrell, Coffee, Poindexter, and Thompson to assemble groups of their own throughout Missouri, but you will report to Colonel Porter if it becomes impossible to reach me directly. He shares my concern about Captain Quantrill."

"Give me command of his troops, General," suggested Slocum. "I'm capable of—"

"Can't be done, Captain Slocum," Hindman said. "There are . . . other matters to be considered." The general's lips moved again, whispering President Davis's name along with a graphic curse. For all Davis's opposition to guerrilla activity, he meddled even here. For whatever reason, the President of the CSA thought more highly of Quantrill than of General Hindman's choices.

"At your orders, sir," Slocum said, standing at attention again.

He saluted and Hindman returned it. He had been given a mission he didn't like, but he was a good soldier. He'd do his best to carry it out for Tom Hindman.

August 11, 1862

William Quantrill lounged back, his gray uniform jacket pulled open. Slocum noted only a pair of silver bars on the newly minted captain's collar. Otherwise, Quantrill had no insignia showing he belonged to the Confederate Army. Glancing around the camp fire, Slocum saw a motley of uniforms—or fragments of uniforms. Most wore what they called a "guerrilla shirt," nothing more than a plainsman's hunting coat cut low in the front and narrowing to a point above the belt where a rosette served as decoration. Four pockets gave ample room for carrying spare ammunition. What startled Slocum the most about the guerrilla shirts was the color. They ranged from a sedate homespun butternut to a brilliant red, hardly the color for a man trying to blend into the countryside. Some even wore captured Union blue jackets. The only two things all shared were a big-brimmed slouch hat and the same number of pistols. No one sported fewer than seven six-shooters.

When they rode into Independence just before dawn, each man would have enough firepower to last through any sustained assault by Spencer-carrying Federal soldiers. Quantrill himself had eight six-guns tucked into belt and bandolier, and Slocum had seen him switch from one pistol to another with greater speed than a soldier could reload any carbine.

"Yes, Slocum, this is perfect, simply perfect." Quantrill's reddish hair shone like spun gold in the firelight. He spoke with a distinct Ohio accent, but none of the men riding with the guerrilla captain took notice of this. He had shown repeatedly how ruthless he was toward Union sympathizers and how relentless he was in pursuit of a column of Federal soldiers, be they infantry, cavalry, or artillery.

The day Slocum had arrived with General Hindman's orders, he had seen Quantrill ride full gallop into the bore of a cannon. Quantrill had fired one pistol until it emptied, switched to another and then another, killing one of the cannon crew and routing the other three. Seldom had Slocum seen such a cold, deliberate attack.

"You up to ridin' with us?" came a shrill voice that set Slocum's nerves on edge. "You don't seem to have the stomach for real battle." Bill Anderson squatted by the fire, eyeing Slocum with obvious distaste.

"I've seen my share of fighting," Slocum said. "Don't much like killing for the sake of killing, though."

"Thought not," Anderson said with a sneer marring his handsome face. "You don't much like the way we have to live or fight."

Slocum didn't reply. Anderson sought to draw him into a fight. Anderson and his partner Little Archie Clement went into battle like Norse berserkers Slocum had heard about. Anderson frothed at the mouth and went totally out of control, killing anything in blue that moved. And Slocum wasn't too sure Bloody Bill Anderson required a Federal uniform in his pistol sights to kill.

Archie Clement was even worse. He rolled up a powerful lot of hatred in such a small, teenaged body.

Slocum sat up, hands near two of his pistols. He could never call these men comrades-in-arms, much less friends. They fought a different battle, one he didn't appreciate. The burden placed on him by General Hindman came down even harder now that a real battle loomed. Slocum wanted to contact Hindman, but Quantrill made sure no one came or left his camp.

That made good military sense to Slocum, but the battle for Independence, Missouri, would be a bloody one.

"Yes, sir, Slocum, this will be a triumph for us," Quantrill rambled on. There was a power to the man Slocum couldn't deny, just as there was a cold heart beating in his breast. He could turn from likeable to brutal in the twinkling of an eye.

"Lookee here. This is the plan for the morning," Quantrill said, motioning to Bill Anderson and Slocum to study the map he sketched in the dirt. "We've joined forces with Upton Hayes, and he tells me that Coffee, Cockrell, and Shelby are moving their cavalry columns northward. We've got damned near five hundred guerrillas in this area." Quantrill's finger stabbed down to the south of Independence.

"Do we wait for Hughes and Thompson to get here?" asked Slocum. "They're supposed to be moving up to Lee's Summit."

"What do we care about them?" demanded Bill Anderson. "We got enough firepower to take that pantywaist holding Independence."

Quantrill nodded agreement. "Buel doesn't know his ass from a hole in the ground. He's only got three hundred men, and Little Archie says they're Second and Seventh Missouri Cavalry along with some elements from the Sixth Missouri Infantry. We met them in the field before and burned their asses good."

Slocum watched as Quantrill continued his sketching. Lieutenant Colonel Buel's men were in an unfortified tent camp a half mile west of the courthouse square. Buel himself stayed in the stone Southern Bank building with a small detachment of guards quartered across the street, and his provost and his guard were at the county jail on North Main Street.

Slocum saw that Buel had isolated himself from his main force. A quick raid, guerrilla style, through the middle of Independence, would bring quick victory. And that was what Quantrill planned. Slocum couldn't have done better, had he been asked for his opinion.

Quantrill told his lieutenants how to deploy their forces for the early morning raid, but he left out Slocum's role. When Anderson and Clement took off to speak with the others, Quantrill turned to Slocum.

"I want you by my side, Slocum. Just this time to see how we operate. No offense meant. You haven't been a Raider long enough."

Slocum said nothing. Quantrill didn't trust him.

"It won't always be like this," Quantrill rambled on. "You riding beside me, I mean. Hell, this is going to be an easy victory, and it isn't going to be that way too often."

"You mean because we always fight forces stronger than our own?" Slocum wasn't sure where the guerrilla leader went with his commentary.

"No, no, Jeff Davis is a fool. The South can't win, and it ought to!" Quantrill's voice rose in pitch, but his pale blue eyes stayed coldly emotionless. "We need to plan for the day when the Confederacy loses—and a real South arises."

"You're planning for that?" Slocum wasn't sure how to interpret what the man was saying. "You reckon the Confederacy will fall and be replaced with something else?"

"They're fools, the lot of them in Richmond. What do they know of war? Yes, the South will come back, stronger than ever. And I'll be there to assume my rightful role." Quantrill took a deep breath and calmed, staring at Slocum as if he had revealed a dark secret. "We'll need money to finance a New South."

Slocum wanted nothing more than to catch a few hours' sleep before the battle, but he felt an obligation to Hindman to find out more of Quantrill's plans. The general had sent him to ride with Quantrill for the purpose of keeping an eye on the volatile guerrilla leader. Something about this talk of a New South sounded to Slocum as if Quantrill's and the Confederacy's aims split and took different roads.

"Don't worry on it, Slocum. Think about the battle."

Slocum lay awake for a few minutes, then drifted off to a troubled sleep. He came awake and sat bolt upright when he heard the neighing of horses. He tried to determine the time from the movement of the stars, but a heavy overcast prevented it.

"Mount up, Slocum," came Bill Anderson's sharp command. "We're ready to give them blue-bellies the what-for!"

Forcing himself to leave behind the comfort of his bedroll, Slocum checked his six-shooters, made sure he had several spare loaded cylinders, and then hefted his saddle over one shoulder. The other members of Quantrill's Raiders were already mounted and ready to fight.

"What's takin' you so long?" asked another of the riders, Joel Mayes by name. Sergeant's stripes shone in bright gold on the man's sleeve.

"You won't leave me behind," Slocum said, getting his saddle cinched down on the fine gray that General

Hindman had furnished him. He swung into the saddle and saw that Quantrill was already on the trail. There wasn't much order to the guerrillas' formation as they rode, but the closer they got to Independence, the tighter the group became.

Almost three hundred men were packed snug as sardines in a tin when they reached the outskirts of Independence. Quantrill rode back and forth, giving last-minute orders.

"I want to hit them where they live. And I want Buel filled with so much lead he'd sink to the bottom of the sea." Quantrill laughed and dispatched several of his lieutenants to get the men into position. Slocum stayed close to the guerrilla leader. Quantrill blossomed, shouting orders and seeming for all the world like the perfect commander. Only the ten pistols thrust into belt and bandolier gave any hint that this was a different military mission.

He drew up next to Slocum and said in a low voice, "There's nothing like a good battle. It makes my blood burn!"

Before Slocum could answer, Quantrill lifted his arm and indicated that they should attack. The ragged line started at a trot and then broke into a full gallop when the buildings at the outskirts of Independence were sighted. The first light of dawn turned the leaden sky into warm pink.

The promise of dawn turned into bloody slaughter as Quantrill's Raiders galloped into town. The few Federals stirring were taken by surprise. Quantrill and Slocum emptied pistol after pistol in the direction of the garrisoned soldiers. Slocum wasn't sure how many bluecoated infantrymen he killed. Four, five, ten—it hardly mattered. He was caught up in the blood lust set free by William Quantrill.

"There's the courthouse, men," shouted Quantrill. "Put the torch to 'er!"

A half dozen firebrands cartwheeled through the air, breaking windows and landing inside the building. Within minutes only a burned-out husk remained. Quantrill had dashed past, not waiting to see the outcome of the fire. The Southern Bank where Buel had garrisoned himself and his guard came in for the next wave of the guerrilla attack. Quantrill reined back in front of the building and fired three pistols' worth of lead into the doors before having to seek shelter from the answering fire.

"They're holed up, Bill," reported Little Archie Clement. "We'll hafta burn the blue cowards out."

"Do it," Quantrill said without hesitation. He kept up a steady covering fire as Little Archie rode past, low in the saddle, and tried to toss a torch inside. The fiery bundle of sticks and pitch fell short, landing on the boardwalk. The stone face deflected the heaviest fire Quantrill's men could put against it, providing a fortress for Buel and his men.

"Damn him. I wanted this to be over quick," Quantrill said. He mustered his men, formed a squad to patrol the streets of Independence, then turned his full attention to routing Buel from the stone fortress.

An hour later he was still firing endless rounds into the building. Worse, Buel's soldiers still returned fire.

"What'll it take to pry him loose?" Quantrill wondered aloud. Slocum saw that Quantrill reveled in the challenge. If Buel had fallen too easily, the guerrilla leader would have been disappointed. For Slocum's part he would have enjoyed having the fight over and done with so he could eat breakfast.

"Captain," Slocum called. "A messenger from Colonel Thompson." Slocum recognized the man's insignia.

"No time for ridiculous self-congratulatory messages," Quantrill snapped. But he took time to listen to the report.

"Sir, we've routed the Federals. They are in full retreat toward Kansas City. But Colonel Thompson wishes to advise you that Colonel Hughes has been killed in action."

"One less sycophant for Jeff Davis to fawn over," snarled Quantrill. "Dismissed."

"Sir, is there a message for Colonel Thompson?"

"Tell him we have taken Independence," Quantrill said. The courier stared at the Southern Bank and the Spencer carbine muzzles poking from the broken windows. Buel was far from defeated. Quantrill turned on the messenger and snapped, "That message and nothing more or I'll gouge out your eyes and cut your tongue from your head. Do you understand?"

"Yes, Captain Quantrill," the soldier said, executing a quick salute. He ran when Quantrill dismissed him.

"How much ammo do they have piled inside?" asked Slocum. "The way those troopers are firing, this might be a major storage area for them."

"Keep up the barrage," Quantrill ordered. "They can't have much more." He began reloading the brace of empty pistols stuck in his belt. Slocum did likewise, astounded that he had expended more than fifty rounds in such a short time.

By the time they had finished reloading, it was past nine o'clock—and James T. Buel waved a white flag.

"Cease firing!" barked Slocum to the guerrillas on his left and right flanks.

"Keep firing!" countered Quantrill. "We accept no surrender. No coward surrenders to *me*!"

"Let me go palaver a spell with them," Slocum asked. "We might be able to move on before noon if we get their surrender."

"We'll kill the whole damned lot of them. No prisoners!" shouted Quantrill. Slocum saw the flash of madness in the man's blue eyes. He had been thwarted and would give no quarter.

A bugle sounded, and Slocum saw a long line of cavalry troopers riding into Independence. At the head of the column rode Colonel Thompson. He dismounted and spoke quietly for several minutes with Quantrill. Then their talk turned into argument. Finally Quantrill angrily pointed at Slocum and said, "Let him be the observer. I want nothing to do with this craven behavior!"

"Captain, come with me," ordered Colonel Thompson. The man stank of gunpowder and had been wounded twice, once in the arm and once in the right side. Slocum knew a soldier when he saw one and immediately followed the colonel.

"How long has Buel been wavin' that white flag?" Thompson asked Slocum.

"Not too long. Maybe since nine o'clock."

"An hour?" Thompson snorted and walked forward, his cavalry saber clanking at his side. He stopped in the middle of the street and beckoned for Buel to exit the Southern Bank. A man dressed only in tight-fitting pants came from the building, favoring his left leg. He saluted the colonel and looked around, as if expecting to be cut down where he stood.

"You are safe under our flag of truce, sir," Thompson said stiffly. "Are you requesting our terms for your surrender?"

"Colonel," Buel said, "we aren't giving up 'less you can promise us we won't be turned over to that bunch of savages." Buel stabbed the air with his index finger, pointing in Quantrill's direction. "They'd line the lot of us up against a wall and slaughter us."

"You have my word as an officer and gentleman, sir, that you will be accorded all the rights of a prisoner of war." The way Thompson said it, Slocum wondered if that included a manservant and fine mansion.

"Accepted," Buel said reluctantly. "I have lost thirty-seven men and have sixty-three wounded."

"The total in your command, sir?" inquired Slocum.

"One hundred fifty."

Slocum backed off, letting Colonel Thompson conduct the formal surrender of Independence. Quantrill's Raiders had broken the back of the Union defenders and assured a quick, if bloody, victory. Slocum mounted and went to find Quantrill.

He paused when he saw Quantrill and his men loading a long line of wagons with loot from the town. Some was left for Colonel Thompson and his recruits, but most was taken by Quantrill for his own purposes.

That night Colonel Thompson marched his men to Blue Springs, and Quantrill's Raiders went hunting for Federal stragglers, killing another forty. Slocum did his part, taking no thrill from it.

4

September 5, 1882

Slocum stared at the copper-haired young woman, wondering if he ought to come right out and call her a liar to her comely face. Deciding he could catch more flies with honey than vinegar, he finally said, "Didn't know Quantrill had a daughter, especially one as lovely as you."

"Why, thank you, John, for such a nice compliment. But you must have met my mother. Kate King, before she married. You might have known her as Kate Clarke." The piercing blue eyes speared him, just as William Quantrill's had so many years earlier. Slocum felt the same cool calculation going on in her head that he had experienced every time Quantrill had spoken to him. Quantrill had seldom shown more than the ice water flowing in his veins.

"Kate King Quantrill," Slocum said, rolling the name across his tongue. It had a strange feel, as if he ought to know it but didn't. He tried to remember Quantrill's escapades with the women and couldn't. Slocum had always wondered about how the cold-blooded killer would go off for days or even weeks on end without telling anyone where he went. He had chewed the fat with the others of Quantrill's Raiders about their leader's absence. Slocum remembered Joel Mayes had been especially fond of conjuring strange liaisons for Quantrill.

Quantrill seemed a poor choice for any decent woman, but there had been rumors. There always were rumors in any military—or paramilitary—outfit.

"Really, John, I'm surprised you don't remember her. Or has that awful Fletcher Taylor tainted your mind with his lies?" The woman batted her long, coppery eyelashes at him, trying to appear coy. She only seemed more conniving to Slocum, a snake eyeing a prospective dinner. "He never much liked Mama, for whatever reason. He called her all sorts of names, none of them true. But then he never did cotton much to my pa, either. They had a big falling out, you know."

All this was news to Slocum. While he had ridden with the guerrilla band, Taylor had been one of Quantrill's most trusted assistants. Slocum might have heard of a feud developing between them, but that had been much later, after Slocum had been gut-shot and was recovering back in Calhoun, Georgia. Slocum's interest in the guerrillas had waned as he put more and more distance between him and their bloodthirsty doings.

"When would I have met her?" Slocum asked. He felt as if he had stepped outside on a nice sunny summer day and unexpectedly found nothing but ice under his boots. Every step he took made him slip a bit more. He thought he had seen a man dead almost twenty years out rustling Double Ought cattle not six hours back. Thinking of Mayes had triggered long-buried memories of that man and the times they'd spent together in the guerrilla unit.

And now this young woman claimed to be the daughter of a man he had nothing but sour feelings about.

"Why, I don't rightly know," said the woman claiming she was Laura Quantrill, her tone prim as any schoolmarm's. "Perhaps on a trip to St. Louis. That was her home."

"Never saw any woman with Quantrill," he said. "He never confided in many of us."

"He always thought highly of Bill Anderson," Laura Quantrill said in her measured tones. "And of you, John. I have his diaries, and I am sure he considered you the cleverest of his men. He wrote so glowingly of your bravery. I have seen that displayed amply tonight. The years haven't taken away one iota of your courage. Why, it was so heroic of you to come to my rescue!"

Slocum had been a spy in Quantrill's ranks, but the guerrilla captain never knew that. His diaries would never hint at what Slocum had really been doing riding with the partisans. At every chance, Slocum had relayed information about the mindless slaughter to General Hindman, even asking the general to trace some of the plunderage Quantrill took from his forays into various Missouri towns. The looting had been extreme in some cases, every business, every bank, every house stripped of anything of value.

Slocum reckoned Quantrill might have been getting rich at the expense of the civilians throughout Missouri and Kansas. He seemed lavish enough with the arms and clothing taken, giving it all to his men. Only when they were fully outfitted did he return it to the families of the men riding with him and of any Southern sympathizers.

But the money, the gold, the valuables stolen in each raid? Slocum had never seen so much as one red cent of it go into the hands of the partisans or civilians who desperately needed it, living as they did under the iron rule of the Federals.

"I just did what any man would," Slocum said. He grew increasingly uneasy at the way Laura Quantrill stared at him. Her eyes never wavered. More and more he felt like a bug being sized up for dinner by a black widow.

"Wait!" she cried, grabbing his arm when he turned to go. "Escort me to my hotel. It is obviously more dangerous on the streets of Kansas City than I'd thought."

He couldn't turn down such a request. He offered her his arm and she took it, clinging tightly.

"You are *so* strong," she said, running her fingers over his upper arm. "You are just what I need." Laura licked her lips seductively and snuggled even closer against Slocum.

"Which hotel?" he asked. He was a little tipsy from the liquor he'd drunk, but he kept his balance well. He knew what the woman wanted and felt more than a little stirring when he looked at her. Laura Quantrill— or whatever her real name might have been—was a powerful pretty woman. Slocum had been on the trail with nothing but the cowboys in the Double Ought crew and a herd of three thousand cattle. The towns they had passed through mostly slammed their doors and kept their women inside until the drovers were past. Only the cow towns like Ellsworth and Dodge and Kansas City welcomed the cowboys with open arms and available women.

But Slocum knew Laura wasn't like that. She wasn't suggesting that he pay for what she had to offer, and this made him even more uncomfortable. Such offers always came with more hooks than a fisherman's creel.

"I'd better go now, ma'am," he said, touching the tip of his hat when Laura stopped outside the Occidental Hotel. It was one of the better hostelries in town, the sort of place he'd expect a well-bred young lady to stay. If he walked into the lobby, there would be unwanted questions asked by the hotel staff. They might even decide to call the sheriff, thinking he was forcing himself on her. Slocum had already gotten his fill of that man.

"You can't," Laura said firmly. "I need to speak to you. It is most fortuitous that we happened to meet tonight. I have a proposal for you." She stared up into his green eyes, her blue ones unrelenting. "A *business* proposal that can make us both fabulously wealthy."

"What might that be, ma'am?" he asked.

"Really, John, you do not have to be that much a gentleman. Call me Laura. We can discuss this inside."

"In the lobby?"

"In my room." She tugged against his arm, but he didn't budge. "Don't worry so about my reputation. This is purely business. Everyone on the hotel staff knows it. I've conducted quite a bit of business since coming to town last week."

Slocum allowed himself to be pulled into the lobby. He didn't like to admit it, but the woman was right. The clerk didn't bat an eye when Laura asked for the key to her room and indicated with a broad gesture that Slocum was accompanying her.

"The city's changed a mite since I was here last," Slocum admitted, climbing the narrow staircase behind Laura. From this angle he enjoyed the view immensely. She had quite a twitch in her derriere, and when she stopped before a door and smiled, he forgot to ask the questions that had come boiling up to the top of his mind. She held the key out to him, her dainty fingers lingering on his as he took it. He put the key into the lock and twisted harder than he had intended.

Slocum wasn't sure what had happened exactly, but the two of them were inside and the door was locked. Laura's shawl was cast aside and the top buttons of her dress were unfastened. He feasted on the view of warm, ample breasts straining to pop free of the fabric. Her arms circled him and drew him close for a quick kiss, then to his surprise, Laura pushed him back.

Slocum fought to keep his balance, almost tumbling over a table at the side of the small hotel room.

"A promise," she said, again running her pink tongue over her lips.

"Of what?" he asked. His tight jeans were getting uncomfortable. Laura noticed and smiled wickedly.

"Of what might come after we talk a little business. John, I need you." She saw the effect this had on him and laughed. "In many ways, I want you. And I certainly need your courage and quick gun." Before Slocum could respond, Laura lowered her voice and bent forward. She said sotto voce, "When you rode with my father you knew he hid away a considerable fortune."

Slocum didn't answer directly. "There always seemed to be wagons of money and supplies vanishing," he said carefully. He was more interested in the way Laura's skirt hiked up when she sat on the soft bed and crossed one slender leg beneath her.

"He knew the Confederacy could never win with a man like Jefferson Davis running things. Davis was a fool, an incompetent. My pa hid all the gold he took from his raids, hoping to finance a New South after Davis was no longer president."

The way Laura spoke, Slocum could hear the ringing promise. The New South.

He was less inclined to think of a new Confederacy rising from the ashes of the old than he was of the woman's nearness. Laura might be Quantrill's flesh and blood. Slocum didn't know. He was too interested in the flesh that was increasingly displayed as she shifted back and forth nervously on the bed. Several more buttons came undone on her blouse, letting her breasts almost fall free from her clothing.

"We can find it, we can forge a new government, we can set the South on the road to independence!" Laura's voice rose from the conspiratorial whisper to a triumphant cry.

Slocum saw her face flush as she warmed to her topic.

"The New South?" he asked, not really listening to her.

"Yes, John, yes! With enough money we can do it. You can be a part. Imagine yourself a senator in the New South." When she saw that this produced no reaction, Laura rushed on: "You can be a governor, be the sole power over tens of thousands of square miles of a new state. You can be governor of the biggest state west of the Mississippi."

"Seems that would tie me down a mite." The spell was being broken. Laura moved on the bed and came closer. He couldn't help noticing her perfume—and the scent of a real, aroused woman. He cared less about political power than the notion he might get rich. That would give real freedom. Slocum could roam at will, doing what he desired.

He knew Quantrill had hidden more than enough gold for a dream like that.

"Wealth, John, wealth and more." Laura's hot breath gusted against his neck. She bent over and lightly kissed his cheek. He felt her tongue moving down the line of his jaw, teasing the hollow of his ear, slipping forward with damp insistence.

"You can be rich," she said in a husky voice, "and you can have me."

She kissed him hard. Slocum returned the kiss with as much fervor as it was given with. He never much believed in treasure maps or lost gold mines. The person doing the selling was the only one likely to make any money. But Laura was willing to give herself freely to him. Slocum knew she couldn't hold him with sex alone and assumed the lovely coppery-haired woman knew that, too.

Right now, they wanted each other. For the moment, that was enough for Slocum. His hands moved down her arms, pulling her blouse as it went. A few buttons popped off as he clumsily opened the blouse to expose frilly undergarments. Slocum twisted around and began kissing the luscious slopes of the breasts he had lusted after earlier.

"Oh, John, you do that so well. I'm all weak and shaky inside." Her fingers fumbled and got his gunbelt off, then struggled with his tight jeans. Slocum found himself occupied trying to figure out the intricate ties and bows on Laura's undergarments. But he succeeded about the same time she got his pants down.

"So big. You're more than a hero, John. You're one hell of a *man*!" She dived down, slipping out of the circle of his arms.

Slocum gasped when he felt the woman's red lips close around the tip of his manhood. She worked on his hard length until he could hardly stand another instant. He laced his fingers through her hair and guided her up and down in a rhythm that set him on fire.

Laura looked up, her eyes dancing with lust. She cupped his balls and gently massaged.

"I want to do more than this, John. Are you ready for me? I'm ready for you. I *want* you more than I can tell you!" Laura swung around, slipping across him. He felt the hardness of her nipples on his chest, and she rolled onto the bed, the springs creaking slightly from their combined weight.

He might have seen a more gorgeous woman, but Slocum couldn't remember when or where. Her large breasts bobbed about gently. Each of the snowy cones was capped with a copper-colored nipple, engorged and pulsing with lust. He tongued first one, then another, but the tides rising within his loins told him he wouldn't find the control to keep going like this much longer.

He had been three months on the trail, and Laura was pretty. Too damned pretty to resist.

"Take me now, John, take me hard!"

Her fingers tightened on his legs, guiding him between her parted thighs. He grunted as his length touched Laura's lust-dampened nether lips. Her fingers cupped his buttocks and pulled him in. He sank balls deep into her yearning interior.

Slocum was surrounded by clinging, moist, hot female flesh. He paused for a moment, staring down into her face. She looked like an angel—or a devil. Laura's eyes opened slightly. Lips parting, her tongue poked through. The view of a woman so locked in passion for him caused Slocum's hidden shaft to twitch.

He began moving, slowly at first to prolong the sensations ripping through him, then with greater speed and power as Laura urged him on. She was gasping and moaning and her body clutched at him.

Slocum slid back and forth faster and faster until he exploded. Laura gasped and began shaking under him. Her body arched as she ground her groin into his, silently demanding ever more. She groaned and bit her lip, shaking like a leaf. Then she sagged back to the bed, gasping for breath. Her eyes opened and she stared at him boldly.

"I knew you were good, John. I just knew it."

She sat up under him and kissed him firmly. "Are you in?"

"Not any more," Slocum said, rolling to one side.

Laura laughed in delight. "You have such a sense of humor. You know what I mean. Can I count on your help?"

"What do you require from me?" Slocum turned cautious again.

"We need men we can depend on, John, and money. We have to reach the vaults. Can we count on you?"

Slocum was familiar with getting a mule to move. If hitting the animal with a stick didn't work, dangling a carrot might. He had just sampled the carrot and been promised more. With it was the promise of immense wealth. Slocum wondered what the stick might be.

"Got to get myself untangled from my job. Folks would talk if I just upped and left. Besides that, they owe me a sizeable wad of money for my efforts." Slocum saw Laura's eyes widen at the mention of money. He wondered what she considered a wad of money. More than he did, Slocum reckoned.

"Good, John, but don't cause any ripples. I'll be in touch. And you can always reach me by leaving a note at the desk. Just address it to Laura, no last name."

"No need advertising what we're doing," Slocum said, getting into his clothing. He was aware that Laura was still naked on the bed. She distracted him every time he moved around to pick up another article of clothing. Her long legs, the reddish patch of fur between them, the large breasts, the way she looked at him as if she were hungry for more.

Slocum knew she was casting her net—and it was working.

"Don't take too long getting out of your job at the Double Ought crew," she said.

Slocum hesitated. He hadn't mentioned whom he worked for, nor had Laura seemed too surprised at seeing him when he came to her rescue. She was mighty familiar, straight out. He began wondering if Laura had ever been in any danger. The window was conveniently placed, and the men were too easily chased off.

He walked through the lobby and out into the warm sun, just poking above the buildings to the east. Slocum sucked in a deep breath of morning air. There was only a faint scent of beeves, and Slocum appreciated that after being on the trail with them so long.

He spun around when he heard the pounding of feet on the boards. Davey Lee Watkins rushed up, out of breath.

"Dammit, Slocum, Horn's been huntin' everywhere for you. Him and Mr. Jefferson and the sheriff."

"Why?" Slocum's eyes narrowed as he studied the man. Something was wrong, and Watkins wasn't hiding it too well.

"You got to get on over to the shack where Horn's waitin' for you."

"You said the sheriff wanted me, too. What's he want to see me for?"

Watkins turned pasty white, and his mouth worked like a fish washed up on the riverbank. The cowpoke tried pointing but only windmilled his arms in a wide circle, totally flustered by the question. This put Slocum on guard.

"Didn't mean nothin' by that. It was just a slip of the tongue, nothin' more, honest, Slocum, honest!" Davey Lee Watkins turned and ran off as if the hounds of hell nipped at his heels. Slocum watched the cowboy vanish down the street and knew that the sheriff wanted him—and it wasn't to ask more damn fool questions.

Kansas City had suddenly become too hot for him to stay, and he wasn't sure why.

5

Slocum ducked into a bookstore when he saw the four men striding along the street, their eyes moving restlessly back and forth. They were out of place on the Kansas City street, and Slocum knew a vigilante when he saw one. These men were hunting for him, and he had barely evaded them, and that only thanks to Davey Lee Watkins's bungled message from Horn Potter. If the cowboy hadn't gotten flustered and said too much, Slocum might have walked into a trap.

As it was, he ran from shadows—and the four vigilantes out in the street.

"What can I do for you, sir?" asked the bespectacled clerk. The white-haired man pushed his glasses up nervously. The likes of Slocum and other cowboys only came into a store like this to shoot it up or cause some other mischief. "Any particular book you're hunting?"

"Newspapers from back East," Slocum said, thinking quickly. "Do you have any?"

"Why, yes, several recent editions came in on yesterday's stagecoach from St. Louis," the man said, brightening. He went to a box and began rummaging through it. Slocum watched with half an eye. His attention was fixed on the four vigilantes outside. The way they kept touching the butts of the six-shooters hanging at their

46

sides, they were definitely stalking someone. Slocum might have thought it was someone else until they went to the hotel where he had spent such a glorious night with Laura Quantrill. Two vigilantes went inside, another stayed outside, and the other went around to the rear. They were out gunning for bear, and Slocum vowed to get the hell out of town.

He knew when he was the hunter and when he was the prey.

"Here are several from St. Louis and one from Detroit that is only a week old." The man held up the slightly yellowed newspapers for Slocum's perusal.

Slocum took the most recent St. Louis newspaper and scanned it quickly. He had no clear idea where he would go when he left Kansas City, but it would be without much money riding in his shirt pocket. St. Louis might be a good place to go, at least for a while.

"No," Slocum said suddenly. He dropped the paper onto the counter next to him and stiffened. His hand went to the ebony handle of his six-gun and sent the proprietor backpedaling, thinking his life was in danger.

"Not the paper I want," Slocum said, trying to calm the man. "Thanks for showing it to me, though." He glanced around and saw the back door. He left that way, walking briskly down the alley in the direction of the stockyards. Stopping only long enough for his horse, Slocum continued toward the yards, riding hard and fast. He wasn't going to let his Double Ought wages go unclaimed. Horn Potter would put them into his own pocket, if he could.

Besides, he was owed. He had worked long, dusty days for that money.

Slocum slowed his pace the closer he got to the shack where the Double Ought foreman worked. Watkins had said the sheriff might be here waiting for him. The vigilantes looked to be out for some reward—or had been riled up by something more than Slocum could reckon without more information.

The flash of sunlight off a badge sent Slocum behind a watering trough. He crawled on hands and knees until he rounded the trough, then made his way to a feed pen where he could hide as the sheriff and his deputy stalked from the yards.

"He's somewhere," the sheriff grumbled. "I feel it in my bones."

"You're never wrong," chimed in the deputy. The sheriff glared at him and lengthened his stride. The deputy had to scramble to keep up. Slocum frowned at the lawman's words. They were hunting someone, and he'd bet all his pay that he knew the name.

But why? Had a wanted poster come to light? Slocum had more than his share, some deserved but not all. He had killed a judge back in Calhoun, Georgia, and had spent a goodly number of years running from it. The judge had taken a fancy to Slocum's Stand, the Slocum family farm. With his parents dead and him still recovering from his wounds, Slocum hadn't been in much condition to argue when the carpetbagger judge had said no taxes had been paid during the war.

The judge and a hired gun had ridden out to seize the farm. Slocum had left behind two fresh graves and a powerful urge from the law to catch a judge killer.

Slocum sidled up behind the shack where Horn Potter stored his gear. Pressing his ear against the thin wood wall, he heard scuffling noises inside as if rats moved about. He worked around until he found a crack between planks. Squinting, Slocum got a view of Horn Potter and Healey sitting inside the shanty. A half-empty bottle of whiskey sat between them on a small crate.

"They'll find the varmint, Horn. Don't go worryin' so about it," advised Healey. He took a deep swig from the bottle, wiped his lips, and put the bottle back. "I'd've preferred to cut the bastard down to size myself, but if the law wants to take care of 'im, let them. It'll save the cost of the ammo."

"You know Slocum," Potter said. He touched the bottle as if to drink, then pushed it in Healey's direction. Slocum had seen the foreman upset before but not like this. Horn Potter's hands shook, and it wasn't from too much rotgut. The man was downright scared.

"I know you don't have anything to worry over," Healey said. He wasn't shy about taking another drink. "Tellin' the sheriff Slocum was the rustler workin' the Double Ought herd ought to keep everyone around these parts jumpin' for a good, long time."

Slocum turned cold inside, his anger mounting. They had sold him out to the sheriff rather than track down the real rustlers. He had a score to settle with both men, but only after he collected his pay.

"I say he got those longhorns back too fast," Potter said. "How'd he know where they went if he wasn't in cahoots with the rustlers?"

"Now, you know the answer to that, Horn. Don't go makin' yourself crazy. Look at the good side of this. You don't have to pay him any wages, and you just might get part of the reward."

Horn Potter laughed uneasily. "I ain't trackin' him down. If the sheriff wants to do the chore, that's his worry. Slocum is a killer. I seen it in his eyes." The foreman took the bottle and swilled on it, standing and moving around as he drank.

Slocum had heard enough. He moved to the door, drew his Colt Navy, and waited for the right moment. When Potter had his back to the door, Slocum moved fast. He slipped inside, swinging hard. The side of his Colt caught Healey on the temple, sending the man stumbling. Healey's head smashed into Potter's bunk, and he lay still.

Potter swung around, in his confusion pointing the whiskey bottle at Slocum instead of the six-gun tucked into his belt. By the time Potter realized his error, it was too late. Slocum had his Colt cocked and pressed hard into the foreman's face.

"Didn't think you'd be seeing me so soon, did you, Potter?"

"Slocum, look, there's some goldanged flap over you. I tole the sheriff that—"

"I ought to blow your brains out," Slocum said coldly. "If you had any, I would. I listened outside. You put the sheriff on my trail. All I did was save Jefferson a passel of money by getting those beeves back from rustlers. Makes me wonder if you might not have something to do with the rustling."

"No, not me. I don't know nothin' about any rustlers." The foreman's hands shook so hard the bottle slid from his fingers and broke on the floor. Whiskey splashed over their boots.

"Pay me what I'm owed and you can go around stealing any cattle you want," Slocum said. "Just remember, I don't take kindly to fools or liars."

"I don't have that kind of money. You know that Mr. Jefferson wanted—"

"I might consider killing you to pay for what I've put up with," Slocum said, as if talking to himself. "But I'd rather have the money. Wasting a bullet on the likes of you and Healey seems a mite too extravagant for me."

"I might have enough. Here, take this." Potter ripped off his shirt pocket pulling out a thin packet of greenbacks. Slocum flipped through them quickly and saw he was still shy of his real wages.

"You owe me more than twenty dollars."

"My gun. Take it. You can get at least that much for it." The man fumbled for his sidearm, and Slocum hit him on the head with the Colt. Horn Potter fell to his knees, sobbing not to be killed.

"I want my pay. I earned it and you won't pay me. Who's the thief?"

Slocum searched Healey, now beginning to stir. He found a thick wad of bills. Slocum took those, knowing he had more than a fair wage for the work he had given the Double Ought. In spite of that, he didn't feel he had been given enough. He pulled Healey's six-shooter from its holster and stuck that into his belt, beside Potter's pistol. For a crazy moment, Slocum remembered riding with Quantrill's Raiders.

They had all carried a half dozen or more six-shooters. He was well on his way to duplicating those days.

"Your boots," Slocum said suddenly. Horn Potter's eyes widened, whether in shock or anger Slocum didn't much care. "Take off your boots. I can use a new pair."

"I paid sixty dollars for these!" cried the foreman. Everyone in the Double Ought company knew how Potter was about his boots. Slocum didn't care much for the fancy hand-tooling, but he wanted to punish Potter. Making him suffer even on a small matter like this pleased him more than it ought to.

"I'll call us even when you take them off and toss the pair over here." Slocum went to the door and chanced a quick look outside. He had a sixth sense that was now warning him he had spent too long badgering Horn Potter. Whether the vigilantes had come into the stockyards or the sheriff had returned, Slocum couldn't say. It might even be the men he had ridden with for three months coming this way.

Whoever it was meant John Slocum no good.

"Take them and be damned!" Potter threw his boots in Slocum's direction.

"Probably already am. Thanks for the boots and pistols," Slocum said to taunt the foreman. He closed the door behind him and hastened away, retracing his path through the stockyards. He slowed when he came to a pen ankle-deep in cattle dung. Slocum heaved the boots as hard as he could to land in the middle of the foul pen. The fancy boots seemed to float for a moment, then sank until they were completely filled with half-liquid, half-solid filth.

"That's him, Sheriff. I see him!" came the warning cry from behind. Slocum whipped about, his hands going for the two six-shooters stuck into his belt. He began firing first left and then right, with an awkward rhythm due to the difficulty of getting his thumbs onto the hammers to cock the six-guns.

But the fusillade he unleashed drove the careless deputy to cover, and that was about all Slocum could have hoped for.

He dashed between the feed pens, seeking his gelding. He was about to swing into the saddle when a bullet tore through the brim of his Stetson. Instead of mounting, Slocum dropped under the horse's belly and used the animal's bulk for a shield.

"Give up, Slocum. We got you."

"What you want me for, Sheriff?" Slocum balanced in his hands the two six-guns he had taken from Healey and Potter. He had six or eight rounds left. That would be enough to shoot his way free, if he chose the right path away from the stockyards. The last thing Slocum wanted to do now was ride into a trap set by the lawman.

"You know what you been up to. Cain't let you keep on. Give up now and I'll promise you a fair trial." The lawman showed himself for a moment, and Slocum knew he wasn't likely to walk away from the stockyards under his own power. The sheriff clutched a scattergun and looked bound and determined to use it.

A glance over his shoulder convinced Slocum he faced only the sheriff and his deputy. The men usually wandering about the feedlots were all hightailing it away from the shooting. They weren't paid enough to get caught in a crossfire between an outlaw and the sheriff.

Nobody else poked up his head to see what was happening, and Slocum took this to mean he faced only two men. He threw himself up and over his saddle. The gelding protested and tried to rear. Slocum started firing, even as he grabbed the reins with a vicious jerk to pull them free from where he had tethered the horse.

Slocum wasn't able to fire accurately, but he forced the sheriff to get off one of his loads of buckshot too fast. The heavy lead tore a path through the air above Slocum's head. He turned the six-shooters in the direction of the deputy, who had put a hole through his wide black hat brim.

The expression on the deputy's face told how unwilling he was to face Slocum. He yelped and dived for cover. Sliding facedown in the muck, the deputy came to rest behind a pile of rails used to mend fences.

By this time Slocum was squirming around to get fully into the saddle. He stayed low and was glad for it when the sheriff unloaded the second barrel of his shotgun. Slocum felt hot lines crossing his back, painfully telling how close the lawman had come to stopping him.

"Come back here, you mangy cayuse!" shouted the sheriff. Slocum heard the clicking of a shotgun breach opening. But the two blasts that followed the reloading fell woefully shy of hitting their target. Slocum had outdistanced the sawed-off shotgun.

"Keep it up, old fellow," Slocum told his horse, leaning forward to pat the animal's straining neck. He wished he had a carrot or lump of sugar to reward the horse, but that would come later, when they were safe. Right now, escape was the only concern. He slowed his pace to keep from killing the horse under him and tried to figure out the best escape route out of Kansas City. He wasn't sure how many men the sheriff might muster for a posse, but he did know he had to keep riding for a long spell to get away from whatever pursuit followed the gunfight with the law.

Staying on the well-traveled roads gave him more speed, but it also increased the risk of being noticed. All the sheriff had to do was find a too-attentive traveler and know he was on the right trail. Although the going was slower, Slocum chose to cut across country. He varied the horse's gait, walking often, then breaking into a brisk trot and sometimes even an all-out gallop for a hundred yards. Then he would slow to a walk to give the gelding a needed rest.

All afternoon Slocum kept up the pace, but he knew he had made a mistake somewhere—or the men on his trail were expert trackers. While his horse drank from a stock tank, Slocum squinted into the sun and saw the dust cloud moving slowly in his direction. There might be a dozen men kicking up so much dust. He hoped it was only a herd of cattle, but he knew it wasn't.

They came too fast and straight in his direction. Any drovers would be heading to Kansas City, not away from it.

"Come on, let's put some more miles behind us," he said to his gray, pulling it away from the tank. The horse protested loudly, wanting to drink until it bloated. Slocum had other ideas, and traveling fast was one of them.

But his ideas evaporated quickly when he saw the dust being kicked up in front of him. He stood in the stirrups and looked to the west. Those riders were narrowing the distance rapidly. Too rapidly for Slocum's taste.

He was trapped between two bands of men making a whale of a stir as they crossed the prairie. They were pushing their horses to the limits of endurance to maintain such speed. Slocum didn't kid himself for a second that it was only coincidence that the two bands were so close to his line of travel.

Turning due north held some promise for his escape, or he might go south, back toward Kansas City, and risk running into another posse. Judging the rate and direction of travel the best he could, Slocum saw that the two companies after him would come together to the north and cut him off. He went south along a narrow, winding dirt path skirting the stock tank he had just used.

Slocum took a chance going back south and immediately regretted it.

"We kin cut you down where you sit or you kin grab a piece of sky," came the cold words.

Slocum saw he had ridden into an ambush. Men in trees on either side of the trail he had chosen lay flat along limbs, rifles trained on him. He considered shooting it out and knew he would be left for the buzzards if he tried.

He lifted his hands in surrender, wondering if he would get a fair trial back in Kansas City.

6

September 6, 1882

"You move a muscle and you'll weigh ten pounds more, all of it in hot lead," came the self-satisfied call from a portly man astride a swaybacked nag. Slocum had seen the man's kind before. He probably spent his days at some tedious job he hated, then drank away the night in a saloon bragging about imagined heroics—or considering how much the hero he could be, *if* the opportunity ever came to him.

Slocum didn't doubt that the capture of the fabulous outlaw John Slocum would be on this man's lips for a long, long time.

"Don't go getting an itchy trigger finger," Slocum said. "I'm not making any move to get away." Slocum knew they had him dead to rights. He just hoped that they didn't have him dead.

"That's good, real good," the vigilante said, but Slocum heard the disgust in the words. The vigilante wanted Slocum to make a play for freedom so he could cut him down. These men were out for blood. Slocum had to keep them from satisfying their thirst, even if it meant going back to Kansas City and the town jail.

"Disarm him, Boll," came a shaky voice. "Don't want him gettin' no ideas, no matter what he says. He looks to be a dangerous one, a real sidewinder."

Slocum was quickly disarmed. For a long moment, no one seemed to know what to do. Slocum had started to tell them to ride back to town when he heard the thunder of hooves. He turned and looked into the dark distance. The dust cloud approached rapidly and soon spun about and parted to show Horn Potter.

The Double Ought foreman reined back, and a broad smile crossed his face when he saw that the posse had captured Slocum.

"Good work, men," Potter hooted. "There'll be a big reward in this for you all. You're heroes." The foreman fought to keep his horse from rearing. Slocum had never thought the man was good in the saddle or out and believed he ought to have been replaced as foreman a long time back.

"What did you tell the sheriff, Potter?" Slocum called. "It's a pack of lies, I'll bet, but—"

"Don't go listenin' to this varmint, men," Potter cut in quickly. "He's the rustler we been lookin' for. He might have told you about fetching back a few head to make himself look innocent, but we got proof. They'll string him up for sure."

Slocum froze when he saw the change in Potter's expression. The delight at seeing Slocum captured by the posse turned into something worse, something more sinister. The foreman puffed himself up and walked his horse closer. He had happened across something he thought was a good idea and was going to put it into action.

"It'd be a shame to waste public money tryin' him," Potter said slowly, working up his courage to propose a killing. "Why not just string him up out here? We got the proof that he's a rustler. What more can any judge want?"

"I dunno," muttered the one who had taken Slocum's six-shooter. "The sheriff said to bring him in, not lynch him. And we ain't seen the evidence you're talkin' about.

That's up to them shysters to argue about, then we can find him guilty and string him up."

"Are you calling me a damned liar?" Potter puffed himself up even more. "Mr. Jefferson, whose beeves have been stolen by this owlhoot, knows he done it. I say, string him up right now!"

Slocum knew how a crowd worked and saw no way to avoid what was to follow. Most of the men in the posse weren't convinced but let themselves be carried along by the few who sought to spill blood. A lariat sailed through the air and fell over Slocum's shoulders.

He tried to pull free but succeeded only in being pulled off his gelding. He crashed hard to the ground. The impact knocked the wind from his lungs. As Slocum lay gasping, Potter consolidated his position as leader of the lynch mob.

"There's a sturdy oak tree yonder. Let's get him over to it. Drag the bastard!"

Slocum had just struggled to his feet when the man who had roped him took off at a brisk trot. Hitting the ground hard, Slocum was dragged behind. He bounced around, trying to avoid the horse's hooves, more unconscious than aware of what was happening.

But he recovered enough when they arrived at the towering tree with its long, spreading limbs. A rope curled up and over the limb, dangling a few feet over Slocum's head. He stared at it with a curious detachment. He knew he was going to get his neck stretched. In his day, he had committed plenty of crimes that the law thought worthy of such an end. The real irony was his innocence in this instance.

He had done nothing, and he couldn't figure out why Potter was so insistent on making him a victim. Slocum tried to talk some sense into the men and found himself jerked to his knees again.

"Get him on his horse. That'll make the fall even better," Potter said. "If you're gonna hang a man, do it right!" He laughed, and a few others shared his enjoyment of the situation. Slocum saw that many in the posse were still undecided about the hanging, but it did him no good until they argued with Potter. Unless a strong leader among their faction rose, they'd all have his blood on their hands.

"I don't care what he says, I haven't rustled any cattle," Slocum called out, vainly hunting for anything that would convince them. "Take me into town for trial. That'll prove—"

He didn't get any farther. Two men hoisted him back into his saddle after cinching down tight the rope around his arms. He fought to get his hands around in front of him so he could free himself, but the lynchers moved too fast. The noose snugged securely on his neck, cutting a deep groove in his flesh.

Slocum stopped fighting to get free and worried more about remaining still to prevent his gelding bolting from under him. Using his knees, he tried to control the nervous animal. The horse was good for cutting calves and rounding up strays. It didn't cotton much to the loud jeers of the lynch mob.

It wanted to take out running—and if it did, its rider would be left dangling by his neck.

"You got this all wrong," Slocum hollered. "I never rustled a single cow from Charles Jefferson or the Double Ought herd. Why is Horn Potter so eager to see me swinging? It's personal between him and me. I never rustled—"

"That's what they all say," the foreman cut in. "Ever hear of a man sent to the gallows who wasn't innocent?" Potter had all the aces in his hand and played them all at once. "Go on, hang him. Get that worthless pile of—"

The shotgun blast ripping through the night caused Slocum's horse to break into a run. For a moment, Slocum wondered what had gone wrong, if this was what it meant to be dead. Hot flashes along the side

of his head burned like a kerosene blaze, and his whole
body felt as if it had been pounded by a bare-knuckles
prizefighter for a hundred rounds.

But he wasn't hanging from the tree limb choking
to death, because Potter hadn't bothered tying a knot
into his noose. Slocum fought to understand what *had*
happened.

The runaway horse was quickly caught and turned
around, pulled to a halt. For the first time, Slocum had
a chance to gather his senses. He blinked hard and saw
a tin star shining in the starlight on a man's chest.

"Never thought I'd be happy to see a deputy," Slocum
said, shaking in an attempt to get the rope around him
free.

"Don't go doin' that, Slocum," came the hard-edged
words. "You only got a reprieve. I reckon we're gonna
swing you sometime soon, but it won't be tonight. The
sheriff's got a bug up his ass about lynch mobs."

The deputy jerked hard on the rope circling Slocum's
shoulders and turned him around. They rode back toward
the lone oak where a dozen men huddled on the ground,
under the guns of the sheriff and two other deputies.

Slocum tossed his head, struggling to breathe. The
noose was still fastened tightly around his throat. As
the ragged end whipped around, he saw it for the first
time. From the wounds on the side of his head it finally
came to him that the sheriff had used a scattergun to cut
the rope. In the shooting, he had done more than sever
the rope; he had also wounded Slocum with one or two
buckshot pellets.

The deputy pulled Slocum's horse to a halt beside the
sheriff. The dour man glared at Slocum, as if telling him
he had better things to do with his nights than tracking
down desperadoes.

"You could have blown my head off with that sawed-
off cannon of yours," Slocum said, indicating the shotgun resting in the crook of the lawman's left arm.

"Might have saved a passel of trouble if'n I done that," the sheriff said. "You're no prize, Slocum, but I follow the law. I'm responsible for keepin' the peace in this county, and by damn that's what I'll do." The sheriff turned and glowered at the posse. "You boys was supposed to fetch him back, not take the law into your own hands."

"Does this mean we don't get paid?" wailed one of the posse. "I never wanted to hang him. It was that fella. Potter!"

The posse started shouting and trying to assign blame. The sheriff tried to hush them and finally fired the second barrel of his scattergun to get silence.

"You ride on back into Kansas City," the sheriff said. "The hunt's over. You'll be paid your dollar for ridin' out tonight. Use it to buy a shot over at the Emporium or somewhere."

This quieted the posse. Slocum saw Horn Potter glaring at him. The foreman mounted his horse and galloped off, ahead of the others. Slocum wondered where the foreman rode, because he wasn't headed back to town.

"He knows more than he's letting on," Slocum said of Potter. But the sheriff paid him no heed. They began the long ride back into Kansas City, and reached the edge of town. Slocum considered his chances and saw no hope for escape. The deputies with the sheriff were too attentive, what with their boss along and puffed up with the capture of a dangerous rustler.

Dismounting, the sheriff finally took off the rope around Slocum's shoulders. The noose remained only a moment longer. As he tugged it free, the sheriff said, "That'll be back in a week, Slocum. The evidence ag'in you is real good."

"It's all trumped up," Slocum protested.

"You'll have your say in court. Get on into the lockup." The sheriff shoved Slocum toward the end cell of six. With two deputies standing behind them with drawn six-shooters, Slocum saw the last chance for escape vanish. He entered the cell and sank down onto the hard cot. Getting out of here would be hard, he saw. Iron bars circled the cage. The only obvious way out was the way he'd entered—through the locked door.

The lawmen left, and Slocum turned his attention to the others in the jailhouse. His eyes narrowed when he saw the man in the adjoining cell.

"Howdy, Cap'n Slocum. Didn't reckon I'd ever see you again," said Joel Mayes.

Slocum didn't answer right away. The man was older than the last time they'd ridden with Quantrill's Raiders—but Slocum had seen Mayes take more than one bullet in the back.

"Surprised to see me alive?" Mayes came to the iron bars separating their cells. He looped his fingers around the bars and leaned closer. "I spent three months recuperating from those Yankee bullets. Never did hear what became of you, because the war was over for me. What happened to you?"

"Didn't come back to Kansas as a cattle rustler," Slocum said. "How long you been rustling beeves?"

Mayes laughed and said, "The same old Slocum. Do you always look at the dark side? I remember once, before we rode into that small town of Federal sympathizers, you wanted to be sure we weren't riding into an ambush. You argued to beat the band with Quantrill. He told you not to be such a pantywaist."

"Seem to remember we did ride into an ambush. Quantrill's informant had been paid off by the Yankee commander."

"See?" Mayes whooped. "Always looking at the back side of every coin, hunting for the counterfeit."

"You in for rustling?" asked Slocum, not caring to hash over the times he'd spent with Quantrill's Raiders. They hadn't been good, and reliving the bloody battles, both won and lost, didn't strike him as a good way to pass the time.

Mayes turned cagey, looking over his shoulder to see if the lawmen might be eavesdropping. He smiled, showing a broken tooth Slocum didn't remember. But the two gold-capped teeth shone brightly in the rear of his mouth, and the scar on his left cheek were exactly as Slocum remembered it. This was the man he had ridden with twenty years back.

"Been doin' a mite of this and that," Mayes said, skirting the answer. "Suppose they got you for stealing cows or you wouldn't have asked."

"I caught you with Double Ought stock," Slocum pointed out.

"You caught me but let me go when you had me in your sights. In the eyes of the law, that makes you an accomplice." Mayes moved along the wall of bars and motioned for Slocum to come closer. Slocum stayed put on the hard cot. Mayes took no notice, but Slocum had to strain to hear the outlaw's lowered voice.

"They got me for drunk and disorderly. I'll be payin' a five-dollar fine in the morning, and I'll be gone. But you're in for hard times, Cap'n. I can tell by the way the sheriff watched you. He thinks you are one desperate hombre."

"I am," Slocum said dryly. He remembered the long hours of jawing with Mayes, mostly to relieve the boredom between fights. Slocum had never much liked the sergeant, but there had been others in Quantrill's Raiders he had disliked even more. Joel Mayes had seemed like an oasis in a desert of vicious killing.

Mayes laughed. "You haven't changed one little bit, Slocum. I can tell. That makes it all the more likely they'll stretch your neck. I've seen 'em around here. Horse stealin' and cattle rustlin' are the two worst crimes. You'd've been better off shootin' the sheriff in the back."

"It's not the sheriff who deserves it," Slocum said. "He's doing his job. It's somebody else." His thoughts wandered to Horn Potter and the man's treachery. As hard as it was for him to believe, Slocum thought the foreman had lied about the rustling simply because Slocum had taken it into his head to collect what was due him.

Or was there more? His thoughts turned down other corridors as Mayes rambled on about Kansas City and its police, the times since the war, riding with the guerrillas.

But Slocum's attention snapped back when he heard Mayes say, "How bad do you want to get out of this cage?"

"What are you suggesting?" Slocum sat up, then went to the bars so the sheriff couldn't overhear by accident.

"Finally got your attention," Mayes said and chuckled. "Well, as I was sayin', I'll be out of here in the morning. They don't want much from me, but you are in for a week of worryin', till the circuit judge comes through. Then they'll be buildin' a gallows just for John Slocum."

"You'd help me get out tomorrow, after they let you out?" Slocum had never felt any loyalty toward Mayes or any of the other guerrillas he'd ridden with. Maybe Mayes thought this was a good way of paying him back for not drilling him when he caught Mayes with the stolen cattle. Or maybe there was more. Strange things had happened since Slocum had come into Kansas City.

"You in or out, if there is a break?" demanded Mayes. The man turned more nervous.

It didn't take Slocum more than a second to say that he was in. Remaining locked up in the calaboose meant a one-way ticket to the cemetery outside town.

"What do I have to do?" Slocum asked.

Mayes didn't answer. He didn't have to. Five masked men burst into the cellblock, six-guns drawn.

7

November 10, 1862

Slocum had grown tired of sewing white death's skulls on his sleeve, one for each confirmed Yankee kill he made. Others in Quantrill's Raiders still festooned their butternut guerrilla shirts with the gruesome symbols of their deadly raids, but the battle of Cane Hill had taken the thrill out of keeping count for Slocum.

He had spent an entire day firing, killing, reloading to kill again. In the heat of the battle, he wasn't even sure he was shooting at only the Federals. The battle had been a confusing one, the hills of Arkansas filled with smoke and fog and blood floating on the air in a gruesome mist. Cavalry charges into the bores of firing cannon and the wild, sad cries of dying men and frightened animals had taken their toll on him. He longed for the serenity of Slocum's Stand far off in Georgia and knew it might as well be on the moon. Too much death and fighting lay between him and the family homestead.

Slocum lay back in the cold, brown grass and stared up into the clear blue winter sky, wondering how such horror could have occurred only the day before and how such calm could have descended. Not even the stench of death lingered. All the bodies had been buried before noon on the day following the battle.

"The dead are real peaceful neighbors," Slocum said

more to himself than to the others lounging near him.

"What's that, Slocum?" called out Joel Mayes. The sergeant had more than two dozen skulls sewn onto his sleeves. He had been among those wondering if he ought to use red cloth skulls to signify five or ten and save himself the trouble of using needle and thread so often. "You thinkin' on adding more Yanks to the ranks of the peaceable?"

"Reckon we will, soon enough. You heard any rumors about the battle?" Slocum wondered if Lieutenant Gregg would lead the guerrillas again. It rankled Slocum that he, as captain, had to ride as an underling to the younger officer, but that was the way brevet ranking worked. Gregg was a West Pointer and trained, or so they said. Slocum's rank was conferred in combat and served only in certain conditions, mostly if anything happened to Gregg.

Slocum snorted at the injustice of the way Jeff Davis insisted on his military being run and found a dried twig to chew on. He wasn't even sure about wanting to lead a cavalry charge. Maybe it was best that Lieutenant Gregg rode up front, an easy target for Yankee sharpshooters with their fine Spencer rifles. Still, if Slocum had to choose which officer to ride behind, William Gregg was a better choice than Quantrill. Their official leader was emotionless in battle, cold-blooded, and never ordered retreat—or quarter. It was best that he was gone, at least for the time being.

Nobody knew what had happened to Quantrill. Off on a secret mission determining the future of the war, Mayes had said. Mayes said a lot of things that nobody knew to be true, just to hear the sound of his own boasting voice. Slocum figured Quantrill might be petitioning General Holmes to expand the partisan war in Missouri—and to wrangle a promotion beyond the rank of captain.

What with General Hindman reduced in power to nothing more than commander of the Arkansas units,

Slocum found himself cast adrift and his secret mission to spy on Quantrill a faintly remembered joke. "Granny Holmes" was an old man, deaf and tired, and not a fit commander for the entire Trans-Mississippi forces. Tom Hindman found himself fighting more political than real battles, trying to hang on to what authority was left him.

Slocum considered Hindman's demotion a pity. Hindman didn't understand that being too aggressive had its drawbacks in Richmond. He had too actively pursued the draft in Arkansas and had been too outspoken an advocate of guerrilla warfare, like that waged by Quantrill. The real tragedy of his demotion lay in the abandonment of plans for an active third front west of the Mississippi that would have kept the Federals jumping. Slocum had heard that Quantrill, Cobb, Porter, Poindexter, and Hays had forced better than sixty thousand bluecoats to chase their own tails in Missouri and weaken their own cause by raping and pillage, even of those civilians supporting the Northern cause.

But those days were gone. And so were Cobb, Poindexter, and Porter, their forces destroyed.

"Yes, sir, the best thing that's happened to us in a fortnight is being assigned to Jo Shelby's Fourth Missouri," Mayes rambled on. He smiled broadly, and Slocum saw two gold teeth shining in the bright sun. Slocum turned away.

"Getting killed under Shelby is no different from getting killed under Gregg," Slocum said. He knew Mayes and Lieutenant Gregg had locked horns more than once. For that matter, the young lieutenant had trouble keeping most of the rowdy guerrillas in line. General Shelby moved fast and knew how to win. Slocum appreciated that, and so did others in Quantrill's Raiders.

"Who's gonna live forever? Now, let me tell you something I heard, Cap'n Slocum," Mayes said, shifting closer. Others nearby pricked up their ears. Mayes was the source of all rumors in the Raiders and always kept them amused with his speculations.

"We're moving out in a while, Mayes," Slocum said. "Make it quick."

"This is a good one, Cap'n. I heard from a sergeant over in Shelby's company that we're being sent back into Missouri to do what we will, that even General McCulloch isn't gonna protest when Quantrill asks for expanded action."

"So we kill more civilians," Slocum said without any rancor. He was sick of going into towns and burning them to the ground, killing anyone foolish enough to stand their ground protecting their homes. The Union commander's General Order Eighteen had established this as the way the war was fought in Kansas, Southern sympathizers—or even suspected sympathizers—having their belongings confiscated and the people sent packing out West. Slocum thought "Old Brains" Halleck wasn't any better than Quantrill, ordering the complete extermination of any guerrilla admitted or suspected.

"Yeah," Mayes said, obviously eager to get more people in his sights. "Anyway, I heard tell we're gonna ride support for Shelby in the comin' fight. The lot of us will support his flank and—"

"Shut your tater trap," came the cold command from Frank James. The guerrilla swaggered over and glared at Mayes. "You know our orders, Sergeant. Don't go mouthin' off. Spies everywhere." James turned his flinty eyes on Slocum, as if daring him to confess to being a Yankee snoop.

"Slocum's one of us, Frank." Mayes swallowed when he saw a half dozen others of Frank James's command coming to back up their leader. "You seen him in battle."

"I have. He fights good enough, but he holds back sometimes. I kin tell."

Slocum pushed to his feet and stared James square in `

the eye. To show any sign of retreat now would mean a bullet in the back of his head. Slocum had enough to contend with dodging Federal bullets without watching his back because he'd tangled with an outlaw turned soldier.

"If the bluecoats don't give you enough fight to keep you occupied, maybe I can oblige," Slocum said. He returned James's hard stare without blinking.

Frank James showed his mercurial nature by suddenly laughing and slapping Slocum on the arm. "You're a pisser, Slocum. You kin ride with me and the boys anytime you want. There'll always be a place for you, no matter what. You got guts."

"I've also got a company of my own to watch after," Slocum said, not exactly speaking the truth. The handful of men under his command had been shot up so badly during the battle of Cane Hill that he was little more than a squad leader now. Some sergeants actually commanded more in the way of troops, but Slocum wasn't pressing the issue too hard. Nobody had ridden through the past few days without losing a friend or two.

"I'll talk to that snot-nose Gregg about integratin' your boys with mine. We'll show the rest of them bastards how to kill." Frank James swaggered away, trailing his men behind.

"We'd better get mounted," Mayes said uneasily, watching James. Slocum had seldom seen Joel Mayes show any fear, but a few of Quantrill's Raiders spooked him something fierce. Frank James was one of them— and Archie Clement another.

For all that, Slocum wasn't too fond of Little Archie or his leader, Bill Anderson. Shrugging it off, Slocum went and corralled his men, got them mounted and into a loose formation. In Quantrill's Raiders they never rode with parade-ground precision, nor was it needed the way they fought. Slocum had no idea what lay ahead. Orders had been sketchy, and he wished Sergeant Mayes had fin-

ished relating the rumors he'd overhead. Slocum knew
nothing about the lay of the land around Prairie Grove
and didn't want to know any more than would keep him
and his men alive through the next few hours. But he'd
have liked to see a map of the area before tearing off to
do battle.

Attacking in the middle of the day seemed odd, but
Slocum had confidence in General Shelby. The man had
shown courage and that he wouldn't needlessly jeop-
ardize his men for the sake of bragging rights to a
questionable victory.

The day drifted by lazily, Slocum hearing distant cannonade but nothing engaging his unit.

Then all hell broke loose.

"Attack!" echoed along the ragged line of cavalry and
partisans.

Slocum passed the command along to those farther
from the line. He recognized Frank James's voice, but
of Lieutenant Gregg or the other officers in the partisan
ranks he saw nothing. Slocum was leery of putting too
much credence in James's order, but he had learned it
was better to act decisively on a stupid order than to
vacillate over the soundest of orders.

His horse lurched, found its gait, and began galloping
forward. Slocum wasn't sure exactly what they attacked.
The thin forest of sweet gum and maple trees showed no
enemy opposition. Quantrill's Raiders blasted through
the wooded area and into a rolling meadow of the purest
green. And here they found immediate action. The Federals had a double line of artillery on the far side of the
meadow, and they charged straight for it.

Chain shot, barrels loaded with bent nails and broken
glass, even regular cannon balls would leave only bloody
memories of them. But the Yankees had their artillery
turned slightly, letting Frank James lead a charge that
was both spectacular and relatively safe.

Slocum ducked low to keep from having his head

shot off by a few Yankee sharpshooters, but the partisans' attack came as a complete surprise for the artillery crews. One officer tried to swing his guns about. But his command came too late.

The partisans hit the line, whooping and firing.

"Get 'em, kill the lot of the bluebellies!" came Joel Mayes's cry from Slocum's right.

Slocum was busy emptying pistol after pistol into the enemy ranks. He rushed forward, bearing down on a young soldier standing his ground. The Yankee had either emptied his rifle or thought it wiser to use his bayonet against a mounted attacker. Slocum flashed past, turning in the saddle to fire repeatedly with two pistols. At least three rounds found the young man's body. He collapsed like a marionette with its strings cut.

And then Slocum rushed past the line and into a heavier wooded area behind enemy lines.

He wheeled around, hunting for new targets. For a moment he couldn't find any.

"Slocum, that you?"

"Here," he answered, recognizing Frank James. "I've lost our line."

"Most got chopped up by them damn Yankees," snarled James, riding over. Behind him came two of his men, shot up. Slocum began to realize how lucky he had been in the attack. Save for the solitary soldier, he hadn't faced any real opposition.

"What are we supposed to do? I never heard from Gregg."

"To hell with that pantywaist," snapped James. "General Shelby's gone and got himself caught in a pocket. The artillery unit we just hit's got his retreat cut off. He was pushin' through to Prairie Grove and ran into more soldiers than you can shake a stick at."

"We can take these artillery soldiers," Slocum quickly decided. "That would relieve the pressure on Shelby's rear."

"To hell with his ass," said James. "We kin drive those bluebellies halfway to the Canadian border if we hit 'em hard enough!"

"Where's the rest of the company?" Slocum asked. "Rally the men, then we can get moving."

"How the hell should I know where they got off to?" James pulled his skittish horse around and headed back toward the enemy lines. The men with him glanced at Slocum, then made up their minds. They followed Frank James.

Slocum had no choice but to join them. Being alone— and a guerrilla—behind Yankee lines was a sure way to end up executed under Halleck's General Order Eighteen. He raced along, switching pistols and getting ready for combat again.

He came across Mayes and a bemused-looking bugler, wearing the tatters of a CSA regular's uniform. Corporal's stripes showed he had been in a few battles, but not enough—or maybe too many.

"You, soldier, sound assembly," Slocum snapped. For a moment the bugler blinked in confusion. He saw Slocum's captain's bars but didn't respond. Slocum had seen enough cases of this kind of shock to know that the soldier was as likely to stand stupidly as he was to obey.

"Do what the cap'n tells you," shouted Joel Mayes, shoving his pistol to the bugler's ear. The soldier gulped, raised the battered instrument, and tried to bugle. Only whistling sounds came out. His mouth was too dry to form the notes.

"Hell and damnation, I kin do better'n that," exclaimed Mayes. The sergeant snatched the bugle from the soldier's shaky hands and put the horn to his lips. Slocum had heard better rallying signals in his day, but this one worked. By twos and threes, Quantrill's Raiders straggled over to join them. As they came, Slocum looked for Lieutenant Gregg but didn't find the officer.

"Where're the others?" he asked after fifty guerrillas had assembled. No one seemed to know. Their orders going into battle had been too vague. Attack and kill was all anyone had been told. Slocum looked to Mayes for the rest of the hearsay he had tried to pass along, but Mayes shook his head.

"General Shelby's got himself in a world of woe," Slocum said. "We have to hit the line of artillery again and let the general slip back." He called over three men, one a sergeant and the other two reliable enough for his purposes. He quickly pointed to the curving line of cannon. They were still leeward of the artillery, but a few crews worked to get their carriages shifted, in spite of officers screaming at them to maintain their murderous barrage of Shelby's troops.

Even one or two cannon might keep Slocum from attacking—and that would doom Shelby.

"Straight ahead, no flagging for any reason," Slocum said, sending the guerrillas on what might be a suicide mission. If what Frank James had said was true, saving Shelby was the only way any of them would ride away from this fight. The general's cavalry formed the backbone of the attack. If it snapped, they all went down to destruction.

Slocum swallowed hard when he saw the leftmost gun turning toward them. There was no more time to waste.

"Forward, attack!" he shouted. He put his spurs to his horse's sides and rocketed ahead of the men, leading the guerrillas into the mouth of the one-inch cannon. The three-pound shell it belched forth could reduce him to bloody tatters. Slocum tried not to think about that as he let out a rebel yell and started firing his pistols with wild abandon.

He reached the edge of the line as the cannon fired. The shock almost knocked him from the saddle. Somehow, although deafened by the roar, Slocum forged on.

He shot two of the artillerists and sent waves of confusion through the others in the crew. And then came the rest of Quantrill's Raiders right behind him. Fifty men burst through the wavering line.

The second gun in the line of artillery turned and fired point-blank. Slocum was past and riding to the third gun, but he knew he'd lost ten men—more—with that single shot. And then all sense of time vanished. He lived, he fired until his six-shooters came up empty, and he switched to another pair.

Only when he had exhausted ten six-guns did he rein back to see what had been accomplished.

The fifty men he had led had been reduced to only fourteen. The toll had been extreme, but the Yankees were in full retreat, leaving behind their artillery, caissons and all. For a moment, Slocum wondered why. The feeble response from the men riding behind him could never have matched the ferocity of the Federal gun crews. Then he turned and saw what he couldn't hear owing to deafness.

Frank James and his men had reached Shelby. The general was retreating along this line, and the sight of the entire Fourth Missouri Confederate Cavalry bearing down on their line had caused the Yankees to break rank and run. Slocum had kept the crews from destroying Shelby's troops as he retreated—and the Confederate general had pulled Slocum's bacon out of the fire.

If either had reacted other than the way he had, both would have been slaughtered by the potent firepower of the heavy artillery.

His once fine uniform ripped and bloody, Jo Shelby rode over and spoke to Slocum. Slocum couldn't understand exactly what the general was saying, but he knew what to do when Shelby thrust out his hand. Slocum shook the general's hand and, through the buzz in his ears, heard, "We've taken the town. Go on in. You've earned it."

Shelby shot Slocum and Frank James a precise salute, then shouted orders to regroup his men. The Federals might have been routed, but Shelby had to keep them running.

"You finally pulled your weight, Slocum. Glad to see it," Slocum heard Frank James say. "We got to get on into town pronto."

Slocum didn't understand what was happening. He was still dazed from the fighting, from the cannon fire, from the deaths. Men from both sides lay piled on the battlefield. It was late afternoon, but before midnight the stench from decaying flesh would be appalling, no matter how cold it got after sundown. Slocum rode along the line of abandoned cannons, knowing Shelby would put the captured guns to good use in other battles.

But where were the partisans going? James had obviously been given orders that Slocum couldn't hear yet.

By the time the remnants of Quantrill's Raiders trotted into the destroyed town of Prairie Grove, the sun had left only bloody fingers in the sky and Slocum heard more than loud ringing in his ears. He kept a sharp eye out for snipers. He had ridden through more than one captured town only to find Yankee sympathizers waiting to potshot any Rebel soldier that came into their sights. Prairie Grove was a Southern town and the battle had been fought to keep it, but that didn't mean a soldier or two might not have been left behind.

"Are we supposed to hold the town?" Slocum asked James.

The man grunted and shook his head. Slocum saw he wasn't going to get any answer from the taciturn Clay County Missourian. The surviving guerrillas slowly drifted into town. Slocum saw William Gregg and almost a hundred men ride in from the east. Where they had been during the battle he couldn't say, but their condition silently bespoke of a hard fight, too. More than five hundred partisans had started the day. Slocum guessed only half would ride on from Prairie Grove.

But the battle had been won. It was a victory. For whom, Slocum couldn't tell.

"There he is, Frank. I see 'im over there by the general store."

Slocum saw one of James's men stabbing with his finger in the direction of the mercantile. A dozen wagons had been pulled up along Prairie Grove's main street. The looting had begun.

And Slocum saw who led the looters. William Quantrill and Little Archie Clement struggled with a heavy iron box they'd removed from Prairie Grove Bank and Trust, an imposing three-story brick structure now set afire. From other stores came those guerrillas closest to Quantrill, all throwing their plunder into wagons.

"To the victor belongs the spoils," Slocum said softly. Then he had to ride hard to keep up with Frank James and the others as they guarded the lead wagon, already pulling away.

8

Slocum looked to Joel Mayes, who smiled broadly. The broken front tooth showed up, as did the gold ones. The scars under his eye turned into a pinkish spider web, giving him a decidedly evil look that did nothing to inspire Slocum's confidence.

"Hey, boys, here I am," called Mayes. One of the masked men pointed in Mayes's direction and whispered a command to the man beside him. The man nodded quickly and fumbled with the ring of keys but didn't go directly to Mayes's cage. Instead, he stuck a metal key into the lock on Slocum's cell.

"Come on," one man said harshly, grabbing Slocum by the arm and yanking him off his cot. Slocum went along willingly. He turned and looked over his shoulder, to call out his thanks to Mayes. Then he clamped his mouth shut tightly. That wasn't too smart. If anything went wrong with the rescue, the sheriff might get wind of Mayes's role in springing him. Slocum decided not to burn a bridge behind him, in case he needed Mayes's help later.

"Where are we going?" asked Slocum. The masked men shoved him roughly through the jailhouse door and into the street. Four more masked men sat astride horses, waiting with Slocum's gelding.

"Get on," ordered the first one.

"What about Mayes?"

"Who? You mean the other one?" This question produced a round of laughter Slocum didn't understand.

Slocum dug his heels in hard and forced the men on either side of him to grab his elbows to keep him moving. Something was going wrong, and Slocum couldn't figure out what it was.

"Who are you?" Slocum demanded, then saw the answer to his question as another masked man rode into view. He recognized Horn Potter's shirt. The Double Ought foreman adjusted his bandanna, momentarily revealing his leering face. Slocum had gone from the lynch rope to jail and had popped back right where he had been out on the prairie.

"We can string him up when we get out of town," Potter said. There was no mistaking the glee in his voice. "Tie him up and let's ride. The sheriff's bound to get wind of the jailbreak any second now."

Slocum stopped fighting and went limp, allowing him to wiggle free of the man on his right arm. Slocum swung around, his fist striking the man on his left hard in the belly. The masked vigilante doubled over, giving Slocum the chance to go for the man's six-shooter.

The sudden wheel of stars and sharp pain told him he had been slugged from behind. Through the haze of pain he heard Potter calling, "Don't buffalo him again. We got to get out of here."

Slocum went where men pushed him, climbing into the saddle. He wobbled as they led him from town. His eyes sent two images to his brain, further confusing him. By the time the pain died and he knew what went on around him, the posse was well outside town.

"Why are you so eager to stretch some hemp around my neck, Potter?" Slocum tried to settle down in his saddle, only to be shoved forward and off balance again by someone behind with a rifle. He didn't fight the muzzle in his back, but took the chance to look around.

Escape looked harder than ever. More than a dozen vigilantes circled him, keeping their distance. If he bolted, they would have him corralled before he got a dozen yards. Still, Slocum had to try if he wanted to stay alive.

He shifted his weight left and tried to get his gelding moving to the right. The feint didn't work. Potter watched him too close. A rope dropped around his shoulders and almost pulled him out of the saddle.

"Go on, Slocum. Do your damnedest," urged Potter. "I'm beginnin' to enjoy this."

Slocum said nothing, as he tried to loosen the lariat around him. But time had run out. They were about a mile outside Kansas City, with only an occasional house along the road. Potter found himself a sturdy, tall cottonwood tree and pointed to it.

"That's the one, boys. We'll string him up there and leave him. That'll keep other rustlers honest, you bet."

A cheer went up. Slocum wasn't sure if the vigilantes were cheering the lynching or the notion his death might deter other cattle rustlers. Whatever prompted their applause, Slocum knew he wouldn't much care. He'd be stone dead.

The circle around him tightened, and the vigilantes moved toward a thick limb. Slocum couldn't help looking up at the sturdy limb and the rope swinging over it. The faint breeze blowing across the prairie carried a hint of fall with it, but Slocum would never enjoy that season or the winter following. He had considered drifting on up to St. Louis or maybe going west to Denver to try his luck. The Rockies with the gold mining camps would have been a real opportunity for someone like John Slocum. Winter always drove the miners into the saloons and made them reckless with their gold dust at the poker tables.

"Hey, y'all over theah. Whatya all doin'?" came a loud question.

"It's the sheriff!" cried one nervous vigilante. "We can still cut Slocum loose and—"

"It's not the sheriff," said Horn Potter. "Do you see any badge? Does that sound like him?"

"But—"

"Shut up!" snapped Potter. "We're within our rights. The *posse comitatus* law says we can do what we want with this cow stealer." Potter turned from his uneasy lynch mob and called to the lone rider, "Get on along. We got serious business here."

"I kin see that," the man said, his Southern accent heavier than ever. "Reckon I got a mite of business with Mr. Slocum mahself."

The first fusillade cut down four of the vigilantes. The second took out another. The rest of the posse, having never been completely sure of their mission, lit out into the night screaming as if a thousand Sioux warriors rode on their heels. With them went Horn Potter. Slocum wasn't sure when the Double Ought foreman cut and ran, but he was glad to see the posse leader go.

But was he any better off? He saw the newcomers riding in. Only four men had driven off three times their number. Slocum glanced at the ground and knew that each of the gunmen coming toward him had killed at least one, shooting the posse members down without quarter.

"No retreat, no quarter," Slocum said.

"You ain't changed so much, Slocum. Not like Mayes said. He said you mighta turned a mite soft." The man laughed harshly, stuffing his two six-guns into his belt. Slocum saw four more guns hanging around the man's body, in the fashion of Quantrill's Raiders. Peering at his rescuer more closely, Slocum saw that the man even wore a guerrilla shirt under a battered canvas duster.

"Don't recognize you," Slocum said. He looked at the other men who had jumped down to strip the corpses of their weapons and other valuables. A fourth man had rounded up the vigilantes' horses. The quick killing had brought a hundred dollars or more to each of the guerrillas, in greenbacks, horseflesh, and loot.

"Joined up after you was shot at Lawrence," came the terse reply. Slocum didn't press the point. He had been gunned down because he hadn't cottoned to the notion of slaughtering boys who wouldn't be men for ten years or more. Slocum had just been rescued from sure death and wasn't inclined to look a gift horse in the mouth.

"You the boys Joel Mayes mentioned?"

"We are, Cap'n," the man said. As his duster flapped open in the breeze, Slocum saw a few medals pinned to the man's shirt. No officer's rank rode on his collars, but he had an air of command about him. Slocum made a few guesses.

"You going to fetch Mayes, Sergeant?" Slocum was glad to see that his assignment of rank had been accurate. The man stiffened slightly and then smiled crookedly.

"Yes, sir, it's bein' taken care of right this minute. Now we gotta ride or we might find a force bigger'n we can handle."

"I doubt that one large enough to give you much trouble exists in Kansas City," Slocum said, meaning it. The firepower carried in these men's belts totaled more than a dozen deputies riding with the sheriff. Even if the lawmen brought repeating rifles, they'd be hard-pressed to fight off a force with such close-up firepower. Quantrill's Raiders had been expert pistoleers, none better—none more deadly.

"This way, Cap'n," the guerrilla sergeant said. He motioned to the others and set off at a brisk trot. Slocum followed, having no better destination in mind. Somehow, he doubted that these men would take kindly to him riding out on his own after they'd gone to the trouble of wasting lead on the posse.

The guerrilla band varied their pace, galloping for a few minutes, then dropping down to a slow walk to rest their horses, then increasing the pace slowly to put the most distance between them and any pursuit. Slocum saw how outriders came and went, scouts hunting for any trace of pursuit. They might even be ordered to erase as much of the real trail as they could or lay false spoor if the sheriff tried tracking them.

Slocum couldn't have done better on his own. He switched from trying to identify the guerrillas with him to studying the stars overhead. The high ice clouds drifting across the sky obscured the Big Dipper and the North Star from time to time, but Slocum got a good idea of where they headed. They rode to the east and north of Kansas City. Slocum had ridden through this country enough times when he'd been with Quantrill, but he didn't know it well.

Damned near twenty years had passed since he'd been a guerrilla fighter. And he couldn't keep the bitter memories of his last days with Quantrill from poisoning his admiration of the way the men around him operated. The war was over, and Slocum wanted it to stay that way.

"We're gettin' real close, Cap'n," the sergeant told him. "Recognize the terrain?"

"Caves?" Slocum had spent many a night in the shelter of limestone caves. Quantrill had favored them as hideouts, but Slocum had never considered seeking them out for his own sanctuary.

"Righto, Cap'n. Y'all jist go on in there." The sergeant pointed to a dark spot. Slocum saw no hint of a cave entrance but dutifully trotted forward. He was never quite sure when he was no longer under the stars but underground. A cold drip or two alerted him to the slow formation of stalactites. The path he followed was well traveled. Countless hooves had cut a deep track, with no attempt made to cover the route.

"Getting too dark to see," Slocum called, aware of men behind him.

As if his words had been heard and heeded, a brilliant flare in front of him momentarily blinded Slocum. His night-adapted eyes saw only dancing yellow and blue dots for an instant, then details took reluctant shape.

A pair of men held blazing torches high over their heads. The thick clouds of black smoke rose to the top of the cavern vault, far higher above his head than Slocum had thought. The limestone caves stretched ahead as far as he could see by the bright illumination.

"The going gets tight, Cap'n," said one man carrying a torch. "Best dismount and lead your horse."

Slocum silently obeyed and squeezed through the ever tighter passage, suddenly coming into a huge room that defied the limits of the lanterns spaced around the chamber.

"Make yourself at home, Cap'n. The others will be here for the meeting anytime now," one of his guides said.

"I can just wander around?" Slocum was startled. He had ridden here with the feeling that any attempt to leave would have been met with blazing pistols. Now he was told he could poke around as much as he wanted.

"Feel free. If y'all want some grub, best head on back to the far side of the room. I got to see to my duties." The man hurried off, leaving Slocum and his horse standing alone at the edge of the room.

Slocum began a slow survey of the room, marveling at the racks of rifles, the kegs of blasting powder and crates of dynamite, the cases of ammunition, even carriages for moving heavy cannon. Of heavy artillery pieces Slocum saw no sign, but supplies to support a full battery throughout a heavy battle were stacked in front of him.

Trying to gauge the scope of the arms he saw, Slocum reckoned a major battle could be fought—or a small war. All that was needed were the men to go into battle.

"Slocum, howdy. Never thought I'd see you again."

Slocum spun, hand going to his empty holster. He relaxed when he saw Ike Berry. And beside him stood David Pool and a man Slocum knew only as Liddell. Memories rushed back, almost staggering him. He wasn't sure if Laura Quantrill was behind assembling the remnants of Quantrill's Raiders, but someone had found the veteran partisans and brought them here.

"Never thought I'd end up here," Slocum allowed. He didn't know what more to say. He wasn't even sure what morass he found himself swimming in. Like himself, these men had been guerrillas and had done their share of killing. They might not have been as vicious as Bloody Bill Anderson or Quantrill himself, but they were still dangerous men. A few years couldn't erase that fact.

"We got to set ourselves down sometime and chew the fat, Slocum," said Berry, "but she's waitin' for you. Over that way. You can't miss it. There's a small chamber off this one she's usin' for a council chamber."

"She?" Slocum shook his head sadly. Berry had to mean Laura Quantrill. "You believe she's who she claims to be?" Slocum had been too occupied lately to think much on the lovely young woman, but now she came back into his life.

Berry thought carefully for a moment, spat, and finally nodded. "She knows enough about Colonel Quantrill to convince me. And the others," Berry added needlessly. Slocum had seen the men with Berry starting to get anxious over his questions.

"That's good enough for me," Slocum lied. He walked across the center of the large limestone vault, seeing even more supplies stashed in niches. It would take Federal commander Major General Curtis's entire force to pry loose even a company of partisans fighting out of this well-supplied armory.

Armory? Fortress.

Slocum looped his gelding's reins over a convenient metal bar driven into the rock and went to the small opening Berry had pointed out to him. A dozen lanterns inside turned the small rock room to day.

"Come in, John. We're about ready to begin. I hoped you would be here in time for our discussion," Laura Quantrill said in greeting. The woman's coppery hair shone like spun gold in the light, and her pale blue eyes might have been chips of polar ice. Slocum hesitated for a moment when he realized he was thinking of her in terms of ice and metal. Even her face looked as if it had been carved from the purest wind-driven snow.

"I'm happy to be anywhere. I reckon it's you I have to thank for rescuing me."

"We can talk about that later," she said, her grin feral. Laura Quantrill took his arm and steered him into the room. At a crude table made of old powder kegs and wood planks sat ten men.

They all appeared more prosperous than Slocum was ever likely to be. Few had missed a meal anytime in their memory, and all were dressed richly, sporting headlight diamond stickpins like gamblers and wearing heavy gold watch chains. More than one chain sported a Masonic insignia or other fraternal emblem.

"I'll introduce you to them later, John," Laura said quickly. "But I think you know some of these fine gentleman already."

Slocum's eyes locked with those of the man seated at the far side of the table.

"Mr. Jefferson and I know one another real well," Slocum said. What was the Double Ought owner doing here, and what was Slocum's part to be? He would find out soon enough. Maybe too soon for his liking.

9

May 5, 1863

The spring flowed into summer, and with it came increasing guerrilla activity. Slocum had lost track of the number of Federal transports they had attacked in the past two weeks. A day back, Quantrill's Raiders had hit a long troop column, charging square through the middle of the Yankees, firing as they went. The troops had been green and had panicked at the sight of so many Rebs riding down on them.

Slocum took no satisfaction with killing untrained soldiers, but it had to be done. Quantrill ordered it—and so did most of the general staff. General McCulloch had been the exception, arguing against partisan fighting. But General Bee, District of the Coast, had praised units like Quantrill's. Even Tom Hindman had found the partisan units useful in keeping the Federals always looking over their shoulders, wondering about the thundering hoofbeats coming up fast from behind.

If they would just get down to a decent fight instead of shooting up freight wagons, it would set a mite better with Slocum. Sitting about and listening to the others brag got boring after a spell.

As if Quantrill were reading his mind, the slender partisan leader marched over and stood in front of a cluster of his officers. His blue eyes worked from one to the other, as if weighing them and finding the lot wanting.

Slocum knew better. They were hard fighting and hard riding, and Quantrill could never get a better crew.

Or a more bloodthirsty one.

"We've got work to do tonight, men," Quantrill said. "No killing necessary, but there's a need for considerable caution. Who's up for it?"

Slocum never volunteered, but now he found Quantrill's eyes boring into his. Slocum nodded slightly, giving the guerrilla leader the sign he wanted.

"Slocum, good. You and Jessup will go out tonight and collect a package from certain parties."

Slocum tensed. He didn't like this part of Quantrill's war plan. He knew what that "package" was likely to be.

"We'll ride together. Bill Anderson and I will go into that town we passed near sundown and conduct our business. It's an enemy stronghold, but we don't have enough men for a frontal assault. We'll sneak in, scout, and be out before they know we're even there."

"The whole area's filthy with Yanks, Major," said Joel Mayes. "I'll ride with you to cover your back."

"Ain't I good enough for that?" snapped Bloody Bill Anderson. The man's eyes took on an eerie yellow aspect in the camp fire–lit night. Slocum remembered seeing starving wolves with eyes like Anderson's.

"Nothing ag'in you, Cap'n," Mayes hastily said. "I was jist pointin' out we're in dangerous country."

"That's all right, Sergeant Mayes," said Quantrill, motioning for his right-hand man to calm down. "*We're* dangerous men. Get mounted. We ride out in ten minutes." Quantrill swung about and marched off, his military manner belying the look of his camp. Four hundred men scattered through the wooded area, in threes and fours, with no one really on sentry duty. They moved too fast for any Union soldiers to catch up with them, or so Quantrill thought.

So far, he had been right. Slocum wondered how much

longer the officer's luck would hold.

He and Sam Jessup rode silently. Slocum never had much to say to the others, nor they to him. That suited him well enough most times, but tonight he was unusually anxious. He knew what Quantrill wanted and didn't think it was any part of war to extort money from wealthy farmers and businessmen. Killing a soldier in combat was one thing, stealing was another.

What bothered Slocum all the more was the destination of the money they were likely to get. Quantrill took it all—and then it simply vanished. After the battle at Prairie Grove, Slocum had seen Quantrill load more than a dozen wagons and drive them off. He had guarded the leading wagon for twenty miles before being ordered back to the unit. From that point on, only Bloody Bill Anderson and Quantrill knew what happened.

Thinking hard, Slocum wasn't sure any of the drivers ever returned.

"Jessup," he said softly enough so Quantrill wouldn't overhear. "You remember George Talley? Wasn't he at Prairie Grove?"

"Might have been. Didn't see him after," the taciturn Jessup allowed.

"I thought he drove a wagon out, one loaded with freight Quantrill took from the town."

"Might have. Seem to remember Talley was a freighter over in Mississippi before the fightin'." Sam Jessup turned a gimlet eye on Slocum. "Why all the questions about Talley?"

"Haven't seen him since he drove off that night."

"Haven't seen a lot of men," Jessup said, settling back into a dour silence that Slocum respected.

They rode another hour before Quantrill motioned them along the dark, deserted road leading to a large farm. This entire area in Missouri harbored Union sympathizers, making their mission all the more difficult. They slowed when they reached the gate leading to the

main house. Off a hundred yards stood a two-story barn.
The winter had been so hard most of the hay to be gone
now, but the farmer had put away enough for his stock
and even had a few new calves lowing in a meadow
nearby.

"You want to talk to the hayseed or want me to do
it?" Jessup pulled a plug of tobacco out of an old leather
pouch and bit off a healthy chew. He contentedly rolled
it around against his cheek, then spat into the darkness. A dog started barking, having finally heard them
approaching.

"I'll talk to the farmer," Slocum said. "Don't go set-
ting any fires unless I tell you."

Jessup nodded and headed for the barn, already
fumbling in his vest pocket for the metal box holding
his lucifers. Slocum wasted no time. If he didn't give
the signal to Jessup quickly, the guerrilla would set
fire to the barn and then get to work on the farmer's
house.

Slocum saw a portly figure come out onto the porch,
draped in heavy shadow. The darkness didn't disguise
the metallic glint of a rifle barrel. Riding slowly, Slocum
endured the yapping dog and the knowledge the farmer
was sighting down the long barrel of his rifle, wondering
if he ought to squeeze the trigger. To him, Slocum was
nothing more than a badger or wolf, just another varmint
sniffing around for whatever it could steal.

Truth to tell, that was about the way Slocum felt.

"Evening," Slocum called. "Reckon you know why
we've come by. Me and my friend out in your barn
want what's due us."

"Thieves!" the farmer exploded. He stepped forward.
Slocum had been right about the rifle. The man waved
it around wildly. This made Slocum more afraid than if
the man had had a cool, steady aim. There was no telling
where a bullet might go.

"This is war, and war's never all neat and tied up

with ribbons," Slocum said. "My commander talked with you—"

"Commander! He's no military man. He's a thief, a sneak thief! He's a damned guerrilla without any standing!"

"Quantrill's talked with you about his due. It'd be a pity to lose that fine barn of yours." As if on cue, a lucifer flared in the night. Jessup held it high, letting the wan light show a pile of hay. All he had to do was drop it and the blaze would consume the farmer's barn and probably spread quickly to his house.

"Extortion, that's all this is! I'm a civilian. All I want to do is live in peace." The whine in the man's tone told Slocum how frightened he was.

"Can't be peace as long as there's a question about states' rights," Slocum said. "I know you lean to supporting the Federals."

"They don't come sniffing around, threatening me."

"You're lucky, then," Slocum said, his voice hardening. He knew any number of equally peaceable farmers the Union forces had stripped of their property and driven off their land simply because they might have been Southern supporters. The stories of what had happened after General Curtis issued his General Order Eighteen had also made quick rounds in the partisan ranks.

Anyone "disloyal" to the Union was to be executed on the spot—and this order was only for show. Curtis himself had said that the guerrillas "deserve no quarters; no terms of civilized warfare. Pursue, strike, and destroy these reptiles . . ."

Peaceable civilians had been massacred under that order. Taking tribute from the Union sympathizers seemed more honorable than killing them outright, as Curtis had ordered his forces to do with Southern supporters.

"We don't have all night, and my friend's fingers might be getting hot from holding that lucifer so long.

You got what Major Quantrill asked for?"

Slocum wasn't surprised to see the farmer lower his rifle and bow his head in dejection. He was paying off an extortionist, and that destroyed his pride. The farmer lifted his eyes a mite and then turned without a word and went into his house. A few minutes later he returned, carrying a heavy leather bag.

"Here, take it and be damned."

"Your curse comes a mite too late," said Slocum, catching the heavy bag. He wanted to look inside, but in the darkness he wouldn't be able to tell what he had. From the bulk, he suspected a considerable amount of gold coin or maybe some gold dust. Where the farmer had found it, Slocum couldn't say. It might be his life's savings, money put away for the day when the crops failed or the plow mule broke a leg.

Now it would go to keeping Quantrill's Raiders in gear for another battle—or would it? Slocum saw a considerable amount of money and goods being taken by the partisan leader and damned little of it filtering back to his men. The guerrillas lived off the land, and by the grace of the few Southern loyalists left in this part of Missouri.

Asking Quantrill where the money went didn't strike Slocum as a good idea, not with the man's cold nature and ability to kill and never show a speck of emotion.

Slocum had started to ride off when the farmer called after him, "When's it going to be? When you coming back to burn me out?"

"Sir," Slocum said, "I'll do my best to keep that from happening. On my word as an officer."

The farmer spat and rushed back into his house. The door slammed and a heavy locking bar fell into place. Slocum reached back and tucked the leather bag into his saddlebags. He had what they'd come for—and he had been summarily dismissed. The farmer didn't believe him, and Slocum couldn't fault him none for that.

But Slocum would try to protect the man's property the best he could. It might not be possible, but the farmer ought to get something for his aid.

"Got all of it, Slocum?" asked Jessup as he rode up.

"In my saddlebags," Slocum said.

"A good night's work, then. Wish I could have burned 'em out, though." And that was all Jessup said as they rode back to camp. Slocum was grateful for the silence since it gave him time to think.

Slocum wondered if Quantrill would notice or care if he took a little of the gold in his saddlebags. The longer he rode the more he thought the guerrilla leader would know. Quantrill didn't miss much—and that meant booty as well as details in his ragtag command.

"Camp," Slocum said, seeing the faint camp fires guttering in the increasingly cold wind. The Cherokees called frosty weather this time of year blackberry winter. Slocum called it damned inconvenient. He pulled up the collar of his guerrilla shirt and tried to ignore the biting breeze seeking to suck away his body warmth.

"You got the loot, Slocum?" demanded Bill Anderson.

"Here it is. Where's Quantrill?"

"He's not back yet. Gimme the bag." Anderson grabbed the heavy bag from Slocum and tugged at the drawstring, opening it enough to peer inside. The man's lips moved as he counted. When he was satisfied all the coins were there, he dropped the bag, catching it by the string so that it closed in one deft movement. Without another word, Bloody Bill Anderson stalked off.

The rumble of a heavy freight wagon caught Slocum's attention. Jessup was unrolling his blanket, getting ready to grab a few hours' sleep before they moved on. Ahead was more riding, more killing, more plundering. Slocum wandered off in the direction of a clump of bushes.

"Where you goin', Slocum?" Jessup demanded.

"To take a leak. Want to hold it for me?"

"Go to hell." Jessup rolled over, the blanket circling

his body. Slocum waited a few minutes, until he heard the dull snores, before pressing on. The shadows gave him a bit of cover, but he was still careful. The guerrillas were always on edge, their trigger fingers willing to curl back and kill anything in front of their six-shooters. A spy sneaking into their camp would be a perfect target for any of the men.

Dropping to one knee, Slocum peered through the undergrowth. Quantrill and Bill Anderson stood next to a battered wagon. Tarpaulins were mounded up in the bed, covering whatever cargo lay there. Little Archie Clement came up and pointed to the wagon. Quantrill shook his head. Slocum grew more curious by the minute. He moved around, hoping to overhear the conversation. He caught only snippets on the wind but got near enough to sneak a look into the wagon.

With Quantrill, Anderson, and Clement at the front of the wagon, Slocum pulled up the tarp at the rear.

He kept from whistling when he saw the dozens of gold bars stowed in the back. Quantrill had stolen a king's ransom from some bank or Union paymaster and carried it in this wagon.

"Get it on out of here, Archie," ordered Quantrill.

Slocum ducked back into shadow in time to keep from being discovered. Little Archie Clement drove the wagon from the camp, but where was he going? Slocum doubted the loot would ever reach Confederacy coffers. He sneaked off, returning to his bedroll. He fell asleep with visions of thousands of dollars in gold being driven into the night.

10

September 7, 1882

"Suffering," one man shouted, pounding his fist on the thick wood plank until it rattled in the small limestone room. "That's what those damned Yankees have brought down on our heads. Reconstruction ruined the South. No day goes by that those Northern carpetbaggers don't flaunt their power and show us the rot in our midst. We cannot tolerate the new laws grinding us down!"

Applause met the man's speech. Slocum didn't know what new laws the well-dressed man spoke of. He paid scant attention to how government ran things. If the law left him alone, he was willing to let the lawmen be. The few times they had crossed swords, such as back in Kansas City, there had been room for Slocum to hie on out and leave behind any problems. He rubbed his neck, remembering how close he had come to being lynched, but that had been instigated by Horn Potter.

His cold green eyes fixed on Charles Jefferson. The man seemed wrapped up in the fine speeches about how the Union still treated the Southerners as second-class citizens. Slocum's problems weren't with the sheriff or town marshal in Kansas City but with the rancher. Potter didn't trot off to the outhouse without Jefferson telling him how and when to go.

"Exciting, isn't it, John?" Laura Quantrill squeezed his arm and looked at him with her piercing gaze. He tried to read what went on behind those enchanting eyes and couldn't. The woman was a complete mystery to him.

"What are they going on about?" he asked her.

"Oppression, how we are being oppressed every day of our lives—and how we can fight back. There will be a new order in the land, John, and it will happen soon. We will fight a new war, and this time we will succeed!"

She made her own fine little speech, but Slocum had heard it all before. The South needed to settle in now, not struggle like a coyote caught in a steel-jawed trap. Chewing off its own leg wouldn't gain anything. The North needed the South's agriculture as much as the South needed the manufactured products produced in the factories scattered across Pennsylvania and Massachusetts.

"Fighting a war takes a heap more than the arms you have stacked out there," Slocum said, jerking his thumb in the direction of the armory. "You'll need men and you'll need money."

"Exactly, John, that's right! You know what we need!" Laura's eyes blazed with fanatical light now. Her grip on his arm kept him from moving away from her. "We can get the men if we have the money, and then everything's within our grasp."

Slocum looked around the table again. The men were prosperous but not well heeled enough to finance a new war. Toss in all their employees, if those men went along with their bosses, and Laura's fine rebellion would still need tens of thousands of soldiers. Wars weren't fought solely with money and arms and matériel. They required troops backed by a dedicated, committed populace.

But these eight men didn't seem to recognize such basic facts.

"How are you planning on taking the fight to the Federals?" Slocum asked loudly, unconsciously falling back into the old habit of calling Northern soldiers Federals.

"We are all pledging ten thousand dollars seed money," Jefferson said pompously. Slocum blinked at the size of the ante. This was one hell of a poker game. "But this is only the beginning. The real money will be delivered later, when it is needed most."

"You've got money like that and yet you try to cheat your drovers out of their pay?" Slocum tried to hold back the fury building inside him.

"I've never done any man out of his due," Charles Jefferson said angrily. "I'm holding back the pay until next week, to keep the men together. I'm willing to offer twice the pay to them to form a company of cavalry riding under the flag of the New South. We just need to make a few more arrangements, then they'll be gainfully employed in the Army of the New South!"

Slocum's fingers tensed into a fist. Jefferson hadn't been square with his men on the trail, and he wasn't now. Slocum heard something more in the rancher's voice that told him Jefferson was as crooked as a dog's hind leg.

"Where's this new money coming from? After the 'seed money' runs out?" Slocum asked.

"Why, I thought Miss Quantrill had told you of our plans," said a man with the look of a banker about him. "Her father's treasure trove will provide the necessary funding to keep us going until the Union capitulates."

This produced a new round of self-congratulatory speeches. Slocum sank back against the cold stone wall, working this over in his head. He had never found out what Quantrill did with the loot taken from the towns, or the extortion money collected, some of it by his own hand. Slocum thought the hiding place had died with William Quantrill when he died of his wounds in the Louisville hospital after being shot in the back.

Bloody Bill Anderson had died months before Quantrill, and only Little Archie Clement had remained of the tight leadership cadre. Slocum struggled to figure out how old Clement had been then. Maybe nineteen, probably eighteen. The fiery youngster could never have held together the guerrillas—but had he known where

Quantrill had stashed all the plunder taken during their campaigns the length and breadth of Missouri?

Slocum doubted it. He turned to study Laura Quantrill's finely chiseled profile—the firm chin and straight nose and soft halo of coppery hair. Where did she figure in on this harebrained scheme? Slocum had never heard Quantrill or any of the others in the rumor-ridden Quantrill's Raiders speak of a daughter. That didn't mean Laura wasn't telling the truth. She looked a powerful lot like William Quantrill, but Slocum needed convincing.

"You know where the booty is stashed?" Slocum asked her. His mind raced. There might be millions of dollars in such a hoard. Quantrill had looted entire towns for most of the war.

"Later, John. We'll talk after the meeting is over."

The fine speeches and arguments over who got what appointment in the New South's government went around the table. It ended with each man accepting some high-blown position and drafting a check for ten thousand dollars. Laura went around the table scooping up the checks, thanking each man personally.

"This will give us a tremendous boost. The guns in the outer cave are only the start. We will begin serious stocking—and then the North shall pay!"

A cheer went up. The men shook hands, congratulating one another, then filtered out through a crevice at the rear of the chamber. Charles Jefferson was the last to leave. He shot Slocum a black look, then vanished through the rock doorway.

"That leads to the other cavern," Laura told him. "They all have special passwords to get past the sentries." The veiled threat held him in his place. Slocum wanted to get out of here now that the lynch mob was taken care of. Then he realized there was a potential for dissension in Laura Quantrill's ranks.

"Your men shot down Charles Jefferson's to rescue me," he told her. "Jefferson's foreman probably got away. When Jefferson comes in with Horn Potter at his side and sees the men who rescued me, hell will be out for lunch."

"You worry too much, John. The men saving your precious neck are all veterans of my papa's unit."

"I recognized them as such," he said. He shivered, and it wasn't just from the dampness in the limestone caverns. He'd never thought to see men the like of Berry and Pool again. After the way he'd parted company with Quantrill's Raiders, he had never wanted to see them again, save at the business end of a shotgun.

"They are loyal. I doubt Charles Jefferson will be able to enlist the aid of many of his men. You know them better than I. Will any of them join the cause?" Her blue eyes bored into him.

Slocum shook his head. The men were drovers, not soldiers, and had no interest in fighting—unless it was in a dance hall over a two-bit whore.

"I thought not, but Jefferson's money will be put to good use." She guided him out of the room, back into the vaulted armory. Slocum couldn't believe this much military ordnance had been moved without someone noticing. The U.S. Cavalry kept close watch on arms shipments, wanting rifles kept out of Indian Territory. The Comanches hadn't been much of a bother lately, but with half the rifles in this room, they'd be on the warpath in a flash.

"Where'd all this come from?" Slocum walked to a box and started to pry the lid off. The markings showed that the crate contained old Enfield rifles, such as those used by the Union troops toward the middle of the war. Laura firmly gripped his arm and pulled him away.

"There'll be plenty of time for that, John. I hope you'll become a major force in the New South. A general, perhaps. Certainly your skill will go a long way toward training green recruits."

Slocum didn't gainsay her belief that he would help. If he wanted out of this armed camp, he had to get past the sentries. Laura had already told him elaborate passwords were needed. From the look of the men patrolling the perimeter of the cave, he wasn't going to get by them with anything less than the right countersign.

"Are those the only men you have financing this venture?"

"You ask such questions, John. No, there are others who share the vision of a New South. We have ambassadors negotiating with Cuba and Mexico now. Those two countries are ripe for an alliance with us."

"What of the Cherokees? I seem to remember that Stand Watie was the last Confederate general to surrender."

"Your memory is good, and we have envoys talking with their principal chief," Laura said in a conspiratorial whisper. "We have so much more to offer them now. They will never be more than wards of the state. We can offer full statehood if they choose it or sovereignty in return for their support."

"Seems those arguments didn't hold much water before. And then most of the Five Civilized Tribes' money was deposited in Southern banks. They stood to lose everything if they didn't cleave with the Confederacy." Slocum eyed the crates as they walked the length of the room, going deeper into the cavern. The bright lantern light faded where the coal oil lamps had been placed farther and farther apart. They finally reached a corridor lit by a single lamp.

"We can convince them. We will, John. We have better people in charge now. Jeff Davis tried to manage every aspect of the Confederacy. It was too much for any one man."

"He was a fool," Slocum said outright.

"Yes, he was," Laura said in a husky whisper. She pushed aside a curtain to reveal a room that had to be hers. A few frilly hangings on the wall took away some of the dampness and made it look like a home. A polished wood table set with knickknacks off to one side would have dominated the room except for the four-poster bed. Slocum let out a low whistle at the sight.

"You surely do know how to rough it," he said.

"I might be giving birth to a new country," Laura Quantrill said softly, moving closer to Slocum, "but there's no need to suffer while I'm doing it. Dreams are better than a rock for a pillow."

She moved closer, her body crushing against his with a growing passion. Slocum didn't hesitate. He remembered the earlier night he'd spent with her and wasn't about to turn down more of the woman's passion. His lips pressed hard into Laura's and his hands roved her fine body. He felt the sleek flow of muscle under his fingers. She was as lithe and fit as a cougar.

Turning slightly so her legs parted, Laura caught his upper thigh between hers. Like a cat, she moved up and down. Rubbing her privates caused her to emit a tiny purring sound.

She tossed her head back and turned her face up to his. The light in her eyes was almost enough to blind Slocum. He wasn't sure if it was ambition or stark lust.

"Take me, John. You're man enough to do it. Take me!"

She tried to spin out of the circle of his arms. He prevented her. Catching her around a trim waist, he hoisted Laura Quantrill into the air and threw her bodily onto the bed. She landed on the soft mattress and sprang to her knees. Slocum dived forward, catching her around the waist again. He bore her backward, but she was fighting him now.

His fingers slid under the woman's blouse. He jerked back, sending buttons flying. He revealed twin mounds of succulent white flesh. For a moment Slocum stopped to savor the sight. This gave the woman time enough to wiggle free. She got her legs up and kicked him like a mule. Slocum tumbled off the bed and onto the hard rock floor.

"If you want me, you have to *take* me," she said, her breath coming in harsh pants now. He saw the red flush rising on her breasts and shoulders and knew she was aroused. She wanted him—if he could catch her.

Slocum discarded his gunbelt and shirt, tossing them aside. He kicked off his boots. The pair watched each other like predator and prey. Slocum wasn't sure which he was as he advanced on her. Laura lashed out, but he batted her hand aside and drove his shoulder into her chest, carrying her full length to the bed.

The woman fought hard, but Slocum was too strong. And he wondered, in some distant corner of his mind, if she really exerted herself fully in repelling his attacks. He got his arm under one leg and lifted, bending her double.

Again he almost lost hold on her. Laura wasn't wearing any of the filly undergarments he'd come to expect. The thatch between her legs was dotted with tiny dewdrops, betraying her kindled passions. He grabbed for and caught that fleecy parcel of feminine territory. His finger slid into her heated interior and wiggled about.

He thought he had grabbed a wild pig. Laura wiggled and squealed and thrashed about. Slocum ducked under a slender leg kicking in the air and positioned himself, using his finger as a guidon. When she relaxed a mite, he moved forward.

His hardness replaced his finger. For a moment, the sudden entry took all the wind from the woman's sails. She gasped and lay back on the bed, a look of stark desire on her face. Then she began arching her back and grinding herself against his groin. Slocum gasped with the intensity of the feelings blasting into his loins.

Laura twisted and turned around his hard length until he wanted to explode.

Grabbing a double handful of ass cheeks, Slocum pulled hard, driving himself balls-deep into the woman. She arched her back even more and let out a shriek that made Slocum worry that guards might come running.

"Don't stop, damn your eyes, don't stop now!" she cried.

Slocum kneaded the handfuls of flesh and began stroking hard, using those convenient handles. Repeatedly he slipped full-bore into her and then slid almost free until the friction burned all along his manhood. When he was sure he couldn't continue another instant, he reached down inside and found a little more control.

Laura shrieked out her lust. Her body responded fully. Slocum felt as if he were being crushed to death in her tight channel. He spilled his seed too fast for his liking, but he lay exhausted beside her on the bed.

Their faces were only inches apart when he said, "That was about the wildest ride I've ever had."

"It's not over, John. It's nowhere near over," she said, swarming over him. Slocum hadn't thought he had it in him to make love again. But with Laura Quantrill's deft urging, he did.

11

The first few hours in the cave had been the best for Slocum. The night spent with Laura Quantrill had tired him out. When he awakened, she was gone from the four-poster bed, and he was on his own. For a week after that he wandered around, aware of the way the others watched him as a hungry snake eyes a bird. He was an outsider, in spite of having ridden with Quantrill. Slocum noted that he was the only survivor of the partisan forces in the cave who had been an officer. The others all had been enlisted men. Slocum didn't know what to make of that. The war had taken a terrible toll, and officers had not been exempt.

An officer riding with Quantrill was especially vulnerable since he usually rode at the forefront of any attack, taking the first bullets. Slocum might have ended up dead because of that, if Bloody Bill Anderson hadn't gut-shot him first. And then only a miracle had saved his life. He had lain ill with the wound and a raging fever for long weeks, barely alive. Only his innate toughness had kept him alive.

Slocum had begun to wonder if he was going to spend the rest of his life underground when Joel Mayes came swinging along, whistling a merry tune.

"Cap'n Slocum, hey, good to see you made it." Mayes slapped him on the back. "I jist knew you weren't gonna end up at the end of any lynch mob's rope."

"You just breeze in?" Slocum wondered if Mayes knew the password to get out. If so, he could wring it from the former partisan sergeant and be gone before anyone noticed.

Before Laura Quantrill noticed, he amended.

"Been outside doin' some scoutin' work. How'd you get away from those vigilantes?"

"Berry, Pool, Liddell, and the others saved my hide," Slocum admitted. "I was about ready to dance a jig in midair when they showed up. They took care of the posse in lickety-split time."

Mayes grinned from ear to ear. Slocum couldn't keep from staring at the broken tooth. Somehow that tooth summed up the way things had gone. A gap, something missing, busted dreams, all that and more—and every bit of it bad.

"Well, Slocum, you ready to earn your keep? I got the robbery all planned out."

"Robbery?" Slocum was puzzled. Laura Quantrill was taking in huge amounts of money from her wealthy backers, and she claimed to know where her father's treasure hoard had been stashed during the years since the war's end. "What are you talking about?"

"A chance to get out of here for a spell," Mayes said. "I don't see why Miss Quantrill wouldn't want you included in the roster. It'll be jist like the old days."

Slocum jumped at the chance to get out of the rock tomb.

"Count me in. What are we going to do?"

"An easy one," bragged Mayes. "A bank. Remember how we rode into Topeka back in '62 and took the town vault apart like a sardine can? They ain't changed that vault in all this time."

"What do we do after we knock over the bank?" Slocum had plans for simply hightailing it, but the details of Laura Quantrill's scheme eluded him. He had no reason to think she wasn't sincere about wanting to see a New South, as she called it repeatedly, but small particulars kept popping up to confuse him. Why risk getting the law down on her with a bank robbery?

"Why, reckon we come on back here," Mayes said, tipping his head to one side and staring curiously at Slocum. "You always was a funny cuss, Slocum. Never knew why Quantrill put up with you,'cept you was one hell of a fighter. A man I'd want at my back, no matter what."

"Thanks for the confidence," Slocum said dryly. "When do we leave?"

"As soon as I roust the others from their bedrolls, we can be on the trail. It's not more'n three days' ride to Topeka, so put up provisions for a week." Mayes swaggered off to get the others. Slocum had seen several men in the cave who were too young to have ridden with Quantrill's Raiders. Mayes ignored them and recruited only from the veterans' ranks. It would be just like the old days, Slocum reflected.

There was likely to be a river of blood flowing when they got to town.

He put together the victuals he'd need, aware that a guard eyed him suspiciously. When he stuffed the provisions in his saddlebags, the guard came over and poked him with the muzzle of his rifle.

"Where do you think you're goin'?"

"He's ridin' with us," came Mayes's cold voice. "You gonna argue about it?"

"Sorry, no. I didn't think—"

"That's your problem. You don't think," Mayes snapped, the old-time sergeant's bark returning to his words. "Cap'n Slocum is one of the finest soldiers in any outfit. You ought to be more respectful."

"But, I was told—"

"Hush your mouth, boy." Mayes stood with his hands resting on two of his six-shooters. The young sentry backed off, suddenly pale. No man in his right mind would quarrel with any of Quantrill's Raiders.

"I'm needing some revolvers of my own," Slocum said. "Should I poke around in the crates and find some?" He had tried several times to look through the armaments crated up in the cavern and had always been denied access. Laura's guards were nothing if not dedicated and damned diligent in the way they kept an eye on the supplies—and Slocum. He wondered how she kept them in line, and if it were anything like the way she sought to pull him into her web.

A youngster right off the range would wrestle grizzlies and bite the heads off rattlers for the approval of a woman as lovely as Laura Quantrill.

"No need. Pool there's got twenty or more six-shooters ready for use. He's our actin' gunsmith." Mayes hesitated a moment, then said, "You were a mighty fair 'smith yourself, weren't you, Slocum?"

"Still am," Slocum said. "When we get back, I'll be glad to lend a hand fixing up any of the firearms." Slocum worried that Mayes might think that Laura had been keeping him unarmed for a reason. That she didn't quite trust him yet would never occur to Joel Mayes, who had ridden with Slocum so many years back.

"They oughta have been keepin' you busy. Gettin' all these rifles in combat condition is gonna take a powerful long time." Mayes made a sweeping gesture encompassing all the rifles in the cavern. He shrugged it off and pointed to the horses.

Slocum was glad to be back on his gelding. The gray settled down under him and felt damned good. Even better were the six six-guns riding in his belt and saddlebags. He had thirty-six quick shots before having to reload, but he would be up against eight other survivors of Quantrill's Raiders. They rode along, showing neither distrust nor real camaraderie with Slocum.

The path out of the limestone cave was straightforward, but Slocum saw the half dozen fortified positions along the route where guards could hold off a small army. Anyone trying to get in—or leave—would find himself arrayed against more firepower than Edward Pickett had faced at Gettysburg trying to break through the Union lines at Cemetery Ridge. More to the point, Mayes rode over to several of the stone redoubts and spoke for several seconds with the guards inside.

He knew the passwords and Slocum didn't. That meant Slocum had to avoid returning. The limestone cavern was as much a jailhouse as anything the sheriff had wanted to lock him in.

"Yes, sir, Slocum, we got a good job ahead of us. The money from them drovers will be in the Topeka bank. That'll go a ways towards financin' our li'l war." Mayes sounded smug about his part in Laura Quantrill's scheme. Slocum rode in silence, wrapped in his own thoughts.

When they camped might be his best chance to simply ride off. Then he touched his shirt pocket and knew he was flat broke. The sheriff had taken the money he'd been paid by Horn Potter—the money he had taken from the Double Ought foreman—and Slocum would find the going difficult without it.

"Money," he mused.

"How's that?" Mayes rode closer, glad for the chance to talk. He was as garrulous as ever and needed an audience for his rumormongering. "You thinkin' on how much we'll make? I reckon it'll be more than a thousand dollars. Might be more, from all the talk driftin' around."

"Do we get a cut?" asked Slocum. "I'm scraping the bottom of the barrel right now." He tapped his shirt pocket to let Mayes know what he meant.

"Reckon Miss Quantrill wouldn't object much if we took a bit of the money to enjoy ourselves—but not in

Topeka," Mayes added quickly. "We might drift through Kansas City and sample some of the whiskey there. And the fillies. Ooeee!" He called. "They surely are pretty there."

Slocum nodded and let Mayes ramble on. Not a woman in Kansas City held a candle to Laura Quantrill. Slocum had been with more than a few women in his day, and none matched the lovely Laura in bed. But he wondered if her skill came from using sex as a tool to get what she wanted. She played a dangerous game assembling the survivors of her father's partisan band. Not a man in Quantrill's Raiders was "safe," and yet she handled them well.

Slocum snorted as he cast a sidelong look at Joel Mayes. Mayes rode off to rob a bank for her and never once asked for a cut of his own. He took the chance of getting killed or caught and never thought of the money. Slocum didn't blame him. The eight men forking over almost a hundred thousand dollars were caught up in the same furor. They argued among themselves over titles and positions in a nonexistent country that Slocum knew could never exist.

The South had fought to become separate, and the mood had been entirely different then from now. Twenty years had changed the country. Slocum didn't know if it was for the best, but he reckoned it was. Slavery hadn't been right; he and his family had never kept slaves. But the fight had been over more than slavery. The Federal government had won out over states' rights advocates, and that was all right by Slocum.

Opening old wounds wasn't likely to do more than leave a passel of men dead and widows crying.

Slocum wanted some of the money from the bank robbery. Even a hundred dollars would get him well on his way toward Denver or Canada or wherever he decided to turn his pony's face. The matter settled in his mind, Slocum rode along and tolerated Mayes and his wild rumors and lewd jokes.

"That's your plan?" Slocum asked in amazement. "Just ride up, walk in, and throw down on them?"

"Why not? They ain't got but a single guard inside the bank," Mayes said, turning irascible. He didn't like Slocum questioning his ability to plan a bank robbery.

"You sure they have all that money inside?"

"Slocum, I *know* it's there."

Slocum eyed Mayes suspiciously. "How's it stored? In gold dust? Bullion? Greenbacks?" He knew the other eight had enough capacity to carry gold bullion, but it would make their getaway more difficult. Slocum began considering how little laying out Mayes had done for the bank heist.

"Jist you wait and see, Slocum. You in or not?"

"Of course I am," Slocum said. He knew he ought to back out now, but to do so meant he'd have to shoot it out with the others. They were committed to a New South, even if he wasn't. Bloody Bill Anderson had shot him for protesting the killing of boys. These men sought the thrill of the old days and wouldn't show any more compunction than had Anderson about cutting down a slacker in their ranks.

"Good. You three stay outside and cover us. The rest of us'll go fetch the money. We're gonna finance an entire battalion with the take!"

"God save us from the zealot," Slocum grumbled as he pulled up his bandanna to cover his face. He drew two six-shooters and put his heels to his horse's flanks. The gelding leapt forward, matching Mayes and the others as they galloped into Topeka.

The bank looked like a crackerbox, but Slocum still worried. The town looked too peaceful, too deserted. Only a few people walked along the street, and they were at the far end away from the bank. Slocum held back for a moment. He had the ugly feeling of walking into an ambush, but Mayes and the others didn't share his suspicions. They jumped from their horses and rushed into the bank.

Slocum was slower to dismount and this saved him.

Gunfire erupted instantly inside—and it wasn't just six-guns. The deep-throated roar of shotguns and the sharper crack of rifles also entered the mix. Slocum kicked the bank doors open and went into a crouch. Two of Quantrill's Raiders lay dead on the floor. Mayes and his partner stood to one side, blazing away.

Slocum took in the trap with a single glance. From behind steel plates came withering fire. Two men with rifles huddled behind the tellers' cages and caught Mayes and the others in a deadly crossfire. Slocum opened up with his two six-shooters, emptying them fast. He tossed the pistols to the floor and drew two more.

"Get out of there," he shouted at Mayes. "They got the drop on us. We can't get to the vault."

"All that money," moaned Mayes. He had been winged at least twice. His left arm was a bloody mess, and he would sport a new scar on his cheek where a bullet had creased him—if he got out alive.

"I'll cover you. Get the hell out of here!" Slocum emptied his second brace of six-shooters and went for the third pair, wishing he had taken even more. The smell of gunpowder, lead, and hot steel filled the bank lobby as Mayes and the other man limped out. They had been shot up but not killed outright. Slocum wasn't sure if that was a boon.

From down the street rode the town marshal with a posse at his heels. They were flinging lead wildly, doing more damage to the town's buildings than to the bank robbers.

"Ride," Slocum snapped. "Get the hell out of town!" He scooped up two fallen six-guns and emptied them in the posse's direction. This slowed their attack but didn't force them to dismount.

Slocum swung into the saddle and bent low, riding for his life. The thunder of hooves behind him told how close the marshal and his deputies were to catching him.

12

"I'll kill the son of a bitch with my bare hands!" Bill Anderson stormed around, his fists thrashing through the air like meaty hammers. "No damned Yankee bluebelly can do this!"

"Bill, calm yourself," William Quantrill told Anderson, as his handsome assistant's face twisted into a mask of stark fury. "We don't know this for sure."

"But, Colonel," said Joel Mayes, "I heard it. Jist as I said earlier, these are the ordinances Tom Ewing has put out."

Slocum sat and listened to the argument and shared some of Anderson's rage. Quantrill's Raiders had never been too upstanding when it came to getting a soldier in gun sights. Kill 'em all, was a typical response when they were asked what they wanted to do to the Federals. And Slocum had swallowed his bile when he was forced by Quantrill to extort money from civilians. If any didn't pony up the money or crops or horses, they were burned out. But they were given a choice. This was war.

At no time in Slocum's memory could he remember any of the partisans intentionally killing a woman or harming a child. The new Union general was changing the rules of the war and changing them for the worse. Since April, when General Ewing took over

112

the District of the Border, he had been arresting and confining women thought to be the wives, mothers, and sisters of the men riding with Quantrill. The bluebelly couldn't catch Quantrill's Raiders so he went after their womenfolk.

From April on Ewing had ordered women picked up in the towns and on farms around Cass, Jackson, and Lafayette counties and taken to Kansas City. If what Mayes said was true, the women had been moved into abandoned hotels and other buildings designated as prisons. What rankled Slocum the most was the vagueness of the crimes charged against the women. Sheltering guerrillas was one thing, if a partisan were caught—or even seen by a reliable witness.

No Union soldier had ever seen any of those women harboring a guerrilla. Quantrill protected the women and made sure the partisans took care of their own. Worse, the women were being arrested on charges as shadowy as buying percussion caps or clothing with stolen money. Slocum knew the women received some of the spoils Quantrill collected, but damned little of it. Wherever the money Quantrill took from his raids went, it wasn't siphoned off to improving the women's lot any more than it was to keeping his troopers armed and in decent uniforms.

"You see the newspaper?" asked Mayes, pulling out a folded newspaper from inside his guerrilla shirt. He shoved it toward Quantrill, who took it and shook the pages open near the camp fire.

Quantrill's expression changed subtly. Slocum had seen the guerrilla leader in the midst of battle, and he never batted an eye. To Quantrill, blood and death were ends to be sought for his enemies. Unlike Bloody Bill Anderson, Quantrill never seemed to take any real pleasure in killing or show much emotion. But he did now.

"Mayes handed me a copy of the *Kansas City Journal*," Quantrill said, choosing his words carefully. "It says the Federals are going to banish all guerrilla families from the state."

"I heard more," Mayes rattled on. He swallowed hard and moved away from Bill Anderson before continuing. "Ewing cain't confine all our families so he's movin' 'em all out west into camps, he calls 'em."

"Prisons, that's what I call them," snarled Bill Anderson. He was working himself up into a killing rage. Slocum knew nothing short of a bullet through the heart was likely to stop Anderson if he took it into his head to begin killing.

"They've killed or run off half of the farmers along the border," Quantrill said, "because they can't find us. They claim the farmers are bushwhacking them. Don't we wish it were so, men?"

"Naw, Colonel," drawled another of the partisans, Berry by name, if Slocum recollected rightly. "I don't want to lose the chance to kill even a single one of them bastards. They're takin' the war to our women. I don't want no sodbuster protectin' those who're under our protection. Makes us look bad. Makes it look like we cain't take care of our own."

"We'll stop them, men," William Quantrill said carefully. "The Federals won't get by with exiling our families, imprisoning our women, making all these wild, false claims."

Slocum said nothing. He knew Ewing had done nothing right since taking over command of the district. One of his first orders had been a declaration that no amnesty be given, either to guerrilla or family, and that prison colonies at Saint Francis and White Rivers, Arkansas, be established. Everything Mayes was relating wasn't news to Slocum—and it was hardly news to the other men. Slocum wondered why Mayes bothered with all this.

Then he found out.

"I got yesterday's paper," Mayes said, his voice shaking. He handed it to Quantrill and then turned tail and ran. Slocum stiffened. Mayes wasn't afraid of anything but Bloody Bill Anderson's wrath. Without even realizing he did it, Slocum's hands rested on the butts of two revolvers.

"Jesus God," muttered Quantrill as he read the newspaper Mayes had given him. His blue eyes turned in Bill Anderson's direction. "Bill, settle down. This is real bad news."

"They got my sisters, don't they?" Anderson asked in a dull voice. For a moment, Slocum felt sorry for the man.

"Worse than that, Bill," Quantrill said. He read the article twice before saying, "They had Josephine, Mary, and Jennie in an old three-story brick building. It collapsed."

"What?" Bill Anderson's eyes shot wide open. For the first time in Slocum's memory the man seemed as if he were chiseled in rock, unmoving and completely beyond emotion.

"Josephine's dead, Bill. Your sister's dead, and Mary is injured real bad. All told, four girls were crushed to death and—" Quantrill was almost bowled over when other partisans rushed forward to read the article over his shoulder.

"By damn, those fiends!" shrieked John McCorkle. "My sister's dead, too! Pa, they done kilt Christie." McCorkle rushed off to find his father to report the death. Slocum held back as a hundred men crowded closer to find out the fates of their loved ones.

Slocum realized Mayes had done right in the way he presented the paper. By starting easy, with outrages they all knew, he had prepared them a little for the bad news. But Quantrill would have a devil of time keeping the men under control now. They'd all demand blood—and Slocum didn't fault any of the men for that.

He saw Cole and James Younger huddled together, tears in their eyes. Two of their cousins had perished.

Then the men left the circle of light, fire in their bellies. Slocum went after them, fearing they would take out their wrath on Joel Mayes. Killing the messenger bringing bad news was a time-honored atrocity. Slocum had no real liking for Mayes, but none of this was the man's fault. He had garnered a reputation as gossip monger and for knowing what others didn't, but this didn't mean he ought to be gunned down.

Slocum found the Youngers with Mayes pinned between them. He held back to watch.

"We want to know it all, Mayes. Don't hold nuthin' back, or I swear, I'll cut your tongue out!" promised Coleman Younger.

"I didn't hear much more'n Quantrill was readin'," Mayes said, but Slocum knew the man was lying through his teeth. There had been more, lots more, and he was hesitant about telling the Youngers.

Mayes grunted in pain when James Younger twisted his arm. Slocum pulled his six-guns but didn't intervene. Not yet, not until they got around to spilling Mayes's blood.

"All right, all right, I'll tell you what I heard. Don't know if it's true, but folks are sayin' that it is." The Youngers released Mayes, who rubbed his shoulder where the pressure had been applied.

Mayes licked his lips and launched into his sordid story. "The women was kept all locked up in a three-story building on Grand Avenue, between Fourteenth and Fifteenth streets. You know the one?"

"Reckon so. They called it the Metropolitan Block, McGee's Addition," said Cole Younger. "It was a falling-down brick building with a liquor store on the first floor."

"That's the one," Mayes said. His eyes darted around. "The women was kept on the second floor. When it collapsed, the crowd jist stood around listenin' to the women scream. Ewing sent in his personal guard company to get them, or so they claim."

"What really happened, Joel?" James Younger never said much, but his cajoling tone carried a world of menace. "You know the real story."

"Rumor has it Ewing had his soldiers remove the support girders so it'd turn into a deadfall. He wanted them women killed, so's it would look like an accident."

The Youngers moved as if a single brain controlled their hands. They drew their six-shooters. Slocum moved in quick.

"Take your anger out on the Federals," Slocum said, one six-shooter aimed at each of the Youngers. His voice brought them back to reality—that Joel Mayes wasn't the one to gun down.

"There's more, ain't there, Mayes? Tell me what it is," asked Cole Younger.

"Ewing's claiming the women brought it on themselves by tryin' to tunnel out. The walls collapsed, he said."

"Tunnel out from a second-floor prison?" Cole Younger turned and stalked off. James Younger followed.

"All hell is turned loose now," Slocum said, knowing the Youngers went back to tell Quantrill—and Bloody Bill Anderson—what Mayes had said. There would be no holding back Quantrill's Raiders now. The war had turned personal for many of the men. Real personal.

"Set fire to the place," James Younger said. Slocum tossed the torch he carried into a haystack. Within minutes, the barn and house were ablaze, black curls of smoke spiraling into the blue sky. The Youngers had already chased off the farmer. His horse crow-footed a little, but Slocum kept it under control.

"Any sign of the patrol?" he asked.

"Don't rightly know, Cap'n, but this much of a fire is gonna draw the bluebellies like moths to a flame." Younger spoke in a dead voice, as he had since hearing

of the deaths of his cousins. Something had died inside
the man, and there had never been too much humanity
in James Younger's breast.

"The others in position?" Slocum was increasingly
nervous about this mission. They had been on a tear
for a week, since hearing of the prison collapse and the
deaths of the women. They had fought and driven off
no fewer than six Yankee patrols, leaving more dead
than Slocum cared to count. In response, General Ewing
had tightened his grip on the territory, driving off more
and more families he thought to be Southern sympathizers.

Slocum wondered at Ewing's intelligence. The man
couldn't think any of Quantrill's Raiders would be
deterred by his reign of terror, especially after killing
so many of their women in his flimsy prison building.
By aiming his soldiers against the civilian population of
Missouri and Kansas, Ewing only made his own grip on
the country more slippery—with innocent blood.

Slocum had heard that Tom Hindman's recruitment
was up fifty percent because of Ewing's atrocities. Now
it was time for Quantrill's Raiders to reduce the number
of troops wearing Yankee uniforms and tip the balance
of power even more in Southern favor.

"We got some company, Cap'n," Younger said,
shielding his eyes against the bright sunlight. He
pointed across a plowed field to the north of the
farmhouse. An entire cavalry company raced for the
burning building, banners flying and bugler tooting a
charge. "See you on the other side of hell!"

Younger wheeled about and galloped off, leaving
Slocum and Joel Mayes behind. Slocum took a deep
breath and waited, pistols drawn.

"We're gonna do it, ain't we, Cap'n?" asked Mayes.
The sergeant ran his thumb over the hammer in a nervous
gesture.

"Don't go firing too quick, Sergeant," Slocum warned.

He judged the distance to be about right. But not yet. Not quite yet.

Then the distance was as he had measured earlier.

"Now, Mayes, let 'em have it now!"

Slocum started firing. He emptied his pistols, stuck them in his belt, and drew two more. He got off eight rounds before the leading element of the cavalry reached a point where Slocum knew hightailing it was better than staying. Slocum called to Mayes, but the sergeant was too intent on shooting at the advancing cavalry.

Wheeling his horse, Slocum reached over and grabbed Mayes's arm.

"We have to get the hell out of here. Now, and that's an order!"

Mayes reluctantly put his heels to his horse's sides. Slocum took off at a gallop down the road, trailing the sergeant. Trees flashed past, and broken fence posts served as markers for how far Slocum had come. The pounding hooves behind him told Slocum how close the entire Federal cavalry was. Their horses were faster, more rested. Inch by inch, minute by minute, they closed the gap.

Hot lead began singing past his head. Bending low, Slocum urged his horse to more speed. The horse failed to respond and began to falter. Its gait turned uneven, and Slocum winced as a bullet grazed his thigh.

"Surrender, damn you!" came the command from the Yankee officer. "Surrender so we can execute you for the traitors you are!"

Slocum would have laughed had his situation not been so serious. Surrender so they could blindfold him and stand him in front of a firing squad? They had to be fools to think he wouldn't die fighting.

Mayes turned and made an obscene gesture. As he turned back, to bend over his horse and get more speed from the straining animal, a bullet caught him smack-dab in the middle of the back. Mayes threw up his arms and took another round.

"Mayes!" cried Slocum, unable to slow his horse. He rushed past the fallen guerrilla, knowing there was no way to save the man. With two shots to the spine, Joel Mayes would be dead. Slocum urged his horse to even more speed.

A side road off the main route beckoned. Slocum used his knees to guide the horse down the peaceful lane even as he turned and began firing. He quickly emptied the second brace of pistols. The cavalry kept after him, getting ever closer.

"Give up, Reb! Give it up or we'll slaughter you!"

Slocum bent over his horse's neck, head low. The horse couldn't gallop any farther. And it didn't have to.

Slocum shot past a small opening in the woods on either side of the lane. Sunlight glinted off dozens of drawn pistols. Then the air filled with leaden death and white gunsmoke as Quantrill's Raiders closed the trap. More than fifty partisans caught the Yankee cavalry in a withering crossfire. Slocum stopped his horse and swung about, intending to join the ambush. There was no need. Only dying moans came from the ambushed soldiers.

They had been wiped out to the man. And even this massacre wasn't enough for most of Quantrill's Raiders. They wanted more death. Lots more.

13

September 17, 1882

No matter the tricks he tried or how hard he rode, Slocum couldn't escape the posse. For a day and a night he had ridden until he was saddle sore and too exhausted to continue. To his gelding's credit, the horse had never flagged once, and only this strength of heart kept Slocum out of the hands of the Topeka marshal.

The gathering thunderheads on the horizon hinted at a heavy late summer storm, but Slocum couldn't count on it to erase his tracks. The marshal had to be part Indian to keep following so diligently after Slocum had dragged brush to erase his tracks, gone up streams and down rocky, dry riverbeds to confuse his trail. He had tried every trick he knew, and still the marshal came after him like some unstoppable, elemental force of nature.

"Drink," he told his tired horse as it bent over a small stream. "We might not get another chance anytime soon." Slocum knew he lied, more to himself than to the gray. The gelding might find itself with a new master, but it would eat and drink and cavort on the prairie. The posse would find Slocum and string him up.

He tried to picture the Topeka bank and how bad the robbery had gone. Joel Mayes had planned it poorly—or not at all. Mayes might have seen the bank and thought the hicks in Topeka could never defend it properly. The promise of large sums hidden away in the vault had blinded the former partisan to the reality of 1882. No marshal let outlaws waltz in and rob his bank.

That they had walked unknowingly into an all-out trap made matters even worse. Deputies had crouched behind steel plates. Slocum had seen that much in the bank lobby. The instant the robbers entered, they'd been cut down without any thought of quarter being offered. How Mayes and Liddell had escaped was beyond Slocum. He had hesitated entering the bank long enough to avoid the first murderous blast from the hidden rifles and shotguns. If it hadn't been for him, Mayes and Liddell would have been buried in some potter's field right now.

That idea didn't trouble Slocum unduly. If he could find Mayes, he'd put the man six feet under. Nothing the former sergeant had done on this robbery had been right. Slocum ought to have demanded a complete plan before getting himself involved in the harebrained scheme. All he had wanted was a few dollars traveling money and he would have been long gone.

Now he couldn't shake the posse so determinedly dogging his every move.

"Enough," he told his gelding, patting the horse on the neck. "Don't want you bloating up on me." The horse needed currying and more than a single bag of grain. That had to wait until Slocum got free of the Kansas law.

If he got free.

He peered up at the thin sliver of argent moon poking above the eastern horizon and tried to gauge the storm track. Getting caught in a Kansas downpour wasn't to his liking, but it would be a damned sight better than rotting in a jail cell. He could dry out. It would take years to get out of a prison cell—or escape a murder charge.

Slocum couldn't remember seeing any of the lawmen bite the dust during the attempted robbery, but the lead had been flying pretty freely. One of the deputies might have taken a slug in the gut. That would explain the marshal's tenacity in tracking him down. A lawman's death could never go unpunished.

Swinging into the saddle, Slocum tried to find the lowest lying ravines to ride through. The moon wasn't too bright, but it might give a pursuer just a hint of silhouette if he weren't careful. Keeping banks on either side of his route struck him as the most sensible course of action to follow.

But in spite of his heedfulness, Slocum rode right up on two deputies crouching by a fire. For a moment it was an even bet who was more startled. Then the lawmen went for their pistols. They had been heating coffee over a low fire made from buffalo chips, and Slocum hadn't seen or smelled the fire.

The lawmen went for their six-shooters, but Slocum was faster. He dragged out two of the revolvers Mayes had outfitted him with and opened fire. The old habits of his days with Quantrill's Raiders returned easily. He didn't fire once or twice, making every shot count. He sent a barrage of lead winging in the deputies' direction, counting more on quantity than quality to carry the day. Slocum winged one deputy, spinning him around to lie moaning facedown on the ground. The other dived for cover behind a nearby rock and gave Slocum the chance he needed to escape.

Instead of reversing direction and galloping off into the night, Slocum urged his horse forward. His gelding trampled the fire and kicked the coffeepot, sending hot liquid spewing in all directions. Bending low, Slocum scooped up the reins of the lawmen's two horses. One nag reared and jerked the bridle out of his hand. The other horse came along docilely enough, at least for the first mile.

When it began balking, Slocum searched the deputy's saddlebags and found a stash of ammunition he could use. A little jerky and a stale hunk of bread completed his newfound treasure.

"Away," Slocum ordered, swatting the rebellious horse on the rump. The deputy's mount reared and then vanished into the darkness. Slocum stared at the ammo and the pathetic handful of food he had taken. Somehow it convinced him he could never get away. He reloaded all his six-guns, but this didn't make him feel any more confident of escape.

Only one sanctuary awaited him. He reluctantly sought the proper star patterns to find his path back to Laura Quantrill's hideout in the caverns.

Slocum grumbled to himself. How *did* the marshal track him in the Kansas drizzle? The humongous rainstorm had never developed. Instead a thin mist had formed, making travel more miserable than difficult. Then the soft rains began, cold and running down his back in icy rivulets. And still the lawman tracked him.

The only consolation Slocum had was the nearness of Laura's hideout. He recognized outjuttings of rock and even found a well-traveled path leading toward the cavern mouth. He shook his head. How she intended the limestone cave to be a lair when she had done everything but put up signposts was beyond him. All Slocum could do was get to the first of the stony guard posts and hope he could convince them he needed asylum.

"There, there he is!" The shout from less than a hundred yards behind him lent urgency to Slocum's flight. A bullet sang through the air, but at this range in the rain no man made anything but a lucky shot. A bolt of lightning in the distance illuminated the gaping mouth of the cavern. Slocum rode right down the middle, not caring if the sentries fired on him or not.

Any gunfire might deter the marshal.

He kept riding until a rocky overhang protected him from the rain. Slocum swung around, determined to make a stand. He had six pistols, all loaded. That would count for something in the fight against however many posse members accompanied the marshal.

Before Slocum could get off a single round, foot-long tongues of flame leapt from a dozen spots along the rocky walls. He dropped to the ground, holding on tightly to his horse's reins to keep the animal from bucking. The echoes rolled and mixed with thunder and the angry shouts from the posse.

"It's a whole damned nest of the vipers," someone snarled. Slocum saw the return fire, but the lawmen had ridden into a trap. As they had been in the Topeka bank, they were now caught in a deadly crossfire. Slocum added a few rounds to the madness, knowing he would never be able to fire accurately. The buck and roar of the six-shooters settled his nerves more than he would have thought. He was finally able to fight back.

And then the marshal was gone. The retreating posse had finally abandoned hope of catching him.

Slocum stood in the center of the path leading into the cave and stared. He had gotten away. Or had he? The lawmen knew where he had run. They wouldn't give up and go home, shaking their heads and telling one another what a pity it was that their suspect had gotten away.

If they couldn't pry Slocum loose from his hidey-hole, they'd fetch the U.S. Cavalry to do it for them. Slocum didn't know that the bank was a federal depository, but it might have been. If there had been even a penny of government money locked up in the vault, the marshal could get an entire cavalry post to come after the robbers.

"So you decided to come home, draggin' your tail 'tween your legs," came a voice Slocum recognized all too well. He spun, six-shooters coming up to cover Joel Mayes. The former partisan stood with his feet planted wide and his hands gripping two pistols. The man's left sleeve had been ripped off and his arm heavily bandaged. Slocum saw a large bloody spot on Mayes's shirtfront where he had taken another round, but other than these obvious injuries, he seemed fit as a fiddle.

"You stupid son of a bitch," Slocum said, raising his six-guns for a quick shot. "You let us ride smack into an ambush."

"That's all right, Slocum," Mayes said, laughing. "You done good. You let us get free by decoyin' the posse away. If it hadn't been for you, the whole danged lot of us would be in jail now."

Slocum's finger tightened, but Mayes didn't see the action in the dim light of the cavern mouth. Slocum heard footsteps behind him as the guards along the walls came into the cave. There wasn't any way he could drill Mayes and hope to get away now. If he had acted quicker, he could have blamed the man's death on the Topeka marshal.

Lowering his guns, Slocum let the men come up behind and slap him on the shoulder, congratulating him for his bravery and selflessness in pulling the posse away from Mayes and the others.

"So how much money did you get away with?" Slocum demanded. "Or was it all for nothing?"

"We didn't get one red cent," Mayes admitted. "But we put the fear of the New South into 'em!"

A cheer went up. Slocum wanted to scream, to start firing and never stop until the last revolver hit a spent cylinder. They were applauding failure. Not only had Mayes failed to get even a worthless federal greenback from the bank, he had forced Slocum to lead the posse right to their doorstep. Now the law knew an outlaw gang hid out in the caverns.

"They'll bring back a cavalry detachment," Slocum said angrily. "They can call up enough men to root us out, no matter what Laura Quantrill has stored down there."

"You think so little of me, John?" came the woman's silky voice. She strode from the depths of the cave, her hips swinging and a smile on her lips that lit up the night. She tossed several bottles of whiskey to the guards.

"Good work, men," she congratulated. "You did yourselves proud tonight. And when they come back with the bluebellies, you'll do even better."

Slocum blinked in surprise. "You *wanted* me to lead the law back here?"

"Not really, but it is giving us a sterling opportunity. My scouts tell me the marshal will find a company of cavalry patrolling less than five miles away."

"Five miles!" raged Slocum. "They'll be back by dawn." He fumbled out his watch and peered at the face. Laura's—and his—survival would be measured in scant hours. If the marshal got lucky and found the cavalry's bivouac right away, they might return within three hours.

"We have a surprise for them, John." Laura shook her head, looking as much like an angel as the devil incarnate. "Come on in and get something to eat."

"Need to tend my horse," he said. The gelding was stalwart and had served him well. Slocum knew he would need the gray's strength again before he won free of this trap.

"Sergeant," barked Laura. "Get someone to tend the colonel's horse." She smiled that wondrous smile again and took Slocum's arm. "See how quickly promotions can come in the New South? You'll be a general before the night is over."

"Rather be a live private than a dead general," Slocum muttered, letting the woman lead him into the cavern. Two youngsters, neither older than eighteen, took his horse and started grooming it. Seeing that they knew their job, Slocum let Laura take him to a mess table. The smell of beans and corn bread, even day-old, made his mouth water. He sat and ate hungrily.

"You have much to learn about strategy, John, but you will learn. You will be one of my finest field commanders."

Slocum didn't reply until he had finished his second helping. For a spell afterward, he refused to talk to Laura about her cockeyed plans for secession. But she managed to turn the conversation back.

"The country is falling apart," she said in her earnest way. "I am only helping it along. Someone must give it order, and I'm that person. With my father's hoard, the dream can become reality."

"Where is this treasure?" asked Slocum. "I rode with Quantrill for years and never knew where he stashed the booty he stole."

"Not stole, John, not that. He was banking it against a different future, a better one than offered by Jeff Davis. The time is ripe for a New South."

"The gold. Where?" he repeated.

"That's one reason I need seed money for the revolt," Laura said honestly. "I have the map but need to find one last landmark before unearthing it all. Then, *then*, the real revolution can commence."

Slocum had started to speak when he heard the cocking of rifles and the clatter of horses in the mouth of the cavern.

"The law. The marshal's back."

Laura smiled wickedly. "I hope he's come with that cavalry detachment." She turned and called out to one of the sentries. Word was relayed back that made Laura smile even more broadly. "I was right. The cavalry accompanied the marshal. Now we shall test the mettle of our troops."

Slocum had started to tell her she had nothing but greenhorns and old men when a cannon drowned out his words. A second cannon blast deafened him. Then he felt only the rumble of the firing through the rock floor. Laura moved closer and held his arm until the barrage died.

"They rode into the mouth of our artillery," she said proudly. "They must have been killed to the man by now."

"You bought field pieces with the money Jefferson and the others gave you?" Slocum knew he was shouting due to his deafness. The ringing in his ears died after a spell, and he could carry on a normal conversation again.

"Oh, yes, part of the money went for our artillery. It was quite necessary that we lure that cavalry detachment into our trap. I am so glad you were the one doing it, John. It reinforces your position among the men as a true leader."

"Why kill them?" he asked, his mind leaping ahead to other possibilities.

"Why, they were the only Union soldiers in the area. With them dead, nothing stands between us and taking Kansas City. In the morning, we ride to begin the new Civil War!"

14

"I won't be denied," insisted Laura Quantrill. "I refuse to wait any longer. We *will* take Kansas City." The woman paced back and forth in the small conference chamber. Her pale eyes flashed angrily, and she tossed her head like a poorly broke filly. Slocum had never seen her lovelier or madder.

After the cavalry had ridden into the mouth of the cavern and been blown away by the field pieces, Laura had thought it would be easy as pie getting an occupation force into Kansas City. She hadn't realized how long it took to mount a real force capable of such a threat. Two days after the cavalry's defeat, she still hadn't formed the force and decided on a reasonable plan.

Slocum kept pointing out how bad the Topeka bank robbery had been because of poor planning. To venture into Kansas City without complete details would be even worse. Having the Topeka marshal after them was one kettle of fish. If they riled enough people in Kansas City, they might have all of Kansas down on their necks.

"Stop it, John. Stop being so negative. We can do it. We *can*," Laura insisted.

"Just pointing out how little we know. For instance, you didn't know that the cavalry post was garrisoned by troopers from Fort Leavenworth. A look at their insignia should have told you that much."

"Fort Kanses," muttered Laura. "We don't occupy Kansas City right away. First, we destroy Fort Kanses."

Slocum closed his eyes and tried not to tell her exactly what he thought of her grandiose schemes of conquest. It was time for him to get away, but he had willingly ridden back into this limestone trap. For all that he had done—or the others thought he had done—on the behalf of the New South, Laura still did not trust him. For this, he had to admit she had a good sense.

"It's an outpost, not a real fort. The soldiers from Leavenworth can supply and reinforce it within days."

"That will be all we need," the coppery-haired woman said with a sureness that almost convinced Slocum. "A victory, one on their ground. That's what we need."

"Why?"

She turned angrily on Slocum, but her expression changed slowly. "Victories win us support."

"You mean more money," Slocum said. "Where is Quantrill's treasure? You said you were still hunting for it. Does that mean you're not sure?"

"I have the map," Laura said. "I need only to find one landmark, the key to the map. When I do, then the entire trove is ours! We will have the resources needed for waging a true war of liberation from Northern oppression."

Slocum had heard her tirade before. He judged how much of this Laura Quantrill truly believed and decided she was driven more by the quest for money than power. And why not? She had almost a hundred thousand dollars from her businessmen supporters. That ought to be enough for any woman—unless Quantrill's treasure trove existed and there was even more hidden there.

Greed had killed more men than Slocum wanted to remember, but he felt the pull of so much wealth tugging at him. He could sneak out of the cavern prison anytime he wanted. All he needed to do was take out one or two sentries and ride out. The marshal might have posted a few scouts outside the cavern, but Slocum had kept ahead of an entire posse getting there. Any watchers might let a solitary rider go, in favor of keeping an eye on the hideout.

"We'll go into Kansas City, John. You and I and a few others from Papa's partisans. I need to talk with our financiers, and coming here is too dangerous for them."

Slocum nodded. He was interested in seeing what message Laura took to her backers. He thought he knew, but going along for the ride could be instructive. If nothing else, it might give him the chance to get away. Even with Mayes and a few others from Quantrill's Raiders at his back, Slocum felt confident enough that he could escape if he wanted.

But the lure of Quantrill's cache proved more and more powerful. He could be rich after only a few minutes stuffing money into his saddlebags.

They rode out of the cave mouth slowly, Slocum at the front and the others immediately behind. He kept an eye peeled for lookouts posted by the law. To his surprise, he didn't see any trace of them.

"We wiped 'em out to the man," Mayes bragged.

Slocum doubted that. Even men riding square into the mouth of a cannon could survive. Minié balls might take off a man's leg, but he could survive. Slocum had seen it often enough during the war. Hadn't Mayes survived two bullets in the back? But this wasn't war and the posse wasn't committed to rooting the outlaws from their cavern stronghold.

Here and there he saw bits of brass from cavalry uniforms and even a bugle, now battered and bent where a frightened horse had stomped on it. The Topeka marshal might have left, but the cavalry would never permit such a slaughter of their patrol. Mayes had claimed an entire company had ridden to their death, but Slocum saw evidence of only a single squad. Even one survivor would take the tale back to Fort Kanses. From there, reinforcements would pour in from Fort Leavenworth, and the fat would be in the fire for Laura Quantrill.

Slocum wondered if Laura worried over the invasion of Kansas City for other reasons. Time was running out for her, and she had to know it.

"We separate and come into town from different directions," Laura said when they neared the outskirts of Kansas City. "Don't get into any trouble that would cause the sheriff to notice you." Laura paused a moment, appraising Slocum. "John, you and Joel come with me."

The look she shot Mayes told Slocum that he was a virtual prisoner, but he didn't consider Mayes much of a threat. He could take the former guerrilla sergeant in any fight, fair or otherwise.

The small group split apart and drifted toward the cow town. With Laura and Mayes on either side, Slocum rode into Kansas City from the south, moving slowly toward the main street. Laura shook her head and pointed to an alley. They took the back ways, avoiding the busier sections where someone might notice them. Slocum appreciated such caution, but he wasn't sure a bolder entry wouldn't pay off for them. One of the vigilantes might remark on their furtive behavior but never notice them in a crowd.

Then again, Slocum had been busted out of the jail and drawn more attention from the law than was healthy.

"Here," Laura said, dismounting behind a two-story brick building. Slocum craned his neck around and caught sight of the edge of a well-kept gilt-edged sign. He had been right about one of Laura's financiers being a banker. They entered the back door and waited for an inner steel door to be unbolted from the inside.

The banker nodded at them and quickly ushered them inside to a tiny room. Laura and the banker took the only chairs, leaving Mayes and Slocum standing behind the woman.

"Good to see you again, Daniel," she said, "but I am disappointed."

"I thought he was good for the money, Laura. Truly, I did. How could I have known the check was no good?"

"You are the banker, Daniel. Your business is knowing such things."

Slocum perked up when he heard the byplay. He thought he knew what was coming—and he did.

"There is no way to collect on Jefferson's check. The man simply doesn't have the money. I wired several banks in Texas. He is broke."

"He has a herd of cattle," she said firmly. "We have a check. Begin legal action to strip him of the longhorns."

"It's not that easy, Laura. He's sold those beeves to packinghouses in Chicago. The cows will be moved out soon. They're fattening for the trip, but—"

"He gave me a bad check. How can we pursue our noble goals now that there is no longer enough money?"

"But it's only ten thousand," the banker protested. "We can get by without his money."

"Artillery is costly. So many items necessary to our preparations are expensive, very expensive." Laura Quantrill launched into a long recitation of reasons she felt betrayed. She ended with "Can we talk with Charles? Perhaps together we can convince him to make the check good."

"He's paid off his hands," the banker said, shaking his head. "He might have some money left, but not ten thousand. Expenses are high in Kansas City feedlots. Without the grain those beeves are eating, the slaughterhouses would never buy Jefferson's cows."

"He forged a bond with us. He agreed to a contract. Is he not a traitor?" Her ire rose and hot spots burned on her cheeks. But Slocum felt a coldness underneath the anger that made him believe this was an act.

"I have business to tend to, Laura. I agree Charles Jefferson is a weak link, but—"

"Why not fetch him here," Laura Quantrill suggested smoothly. "Let us use your rooms upstairs for a more private conference with him."

Slocum wondered at these rooms. The banker gobbled like a turkey and his dewlaps bounced. He finally gave in with ill-concealed indignation.

"Joel, John, find Mr. Jefferson and bring him here. Don't forget, he is still a valued member of our effort," Laura said softly after the banker left.

Slocum figured that either Jefferson's money was necessary for Laura's schemes or she was getting greedy. Ten thousand was a powerful lot of money to lose, but she stood to control vast amounts more if her story about a map showing where William Quantrill's hoard lay was true.

"We'll go get 'im," Mayes promised. He punched Slocum in the arm and started from the small room. Slocum trailed behind, mind working hard. Vast amounts of money flowed through the woman's hands. She might not be as interested in squeezing the money from Jefferson as she was in maintaining her position of power.

"This is going to be hard to do," Slocum told Mayes.

"What? Why's that, Cap'n? All we got to do is go over to the feedlot and find the varmint. Then—"

"You know how I locked horns with his foreman. If Horn Potter catches sight of me, there won't be any chance of getting to his boss."

"You two really don't cotton much to one another, do you?" mused Mayes. "Any reason why?"

"I suspect Potter of rustling from the Double Ought herd and think I can prove it." Slocum stared hard at Mayes. He had caught Mayes rustling from the same herd.

Joel Mayes laughed. "Hell, everybody's stealin' from that herd. We was eatin' real good from the beeves we took. But you're right. Why don't you hang back and let me go fetch Jefferson?"

"I'll back you up," Slocum said. Mayes nodded and started off, trusting Slocum not to hightail it. Slocum realized that some among the veterans of Quantrill's Raiders thought him to be one of them, and Mayes was foremost.

Mayes vanished down the alley on his way to the pens, and Slocum fell behind, slowing down until he came to a halt behind a print shop. Mayes was long gone, and Slocum could have left Kansas City without opposition, but curiosity now held him. He ducked into the print shop and poked around.

"You print the newspaper?" he asked a printer's devil. The boy looked up from his typesetting, dark ink smeared on his cheek, and nodded.

"One of them, mister. What you need? We can do 'bout any job, but you hafta see the owner. He's out right now."

"I'd like to look over back issues of your paper."

"Sure. Over there. Those big leather-bound volumes. Goes back 'bout four years, as long as we've been in business. 'Fore that another company printed the paper."

Slocum let the boy rattle on as he went to the volumes. He hardly knew where to start, so he pulled a year-old volume from the shelf. He sat and began flipping through the pages, not knowing exactly what he sought. The first volume held nothing of interest, nor did the second. But a paper from three years back caught his attention.

He read slowly, taking in all the details of how a young girl had breezed through town and been arrested at Fort Hays for running a confidence scheme. She had sold fake claims to gold mines in Denver. Another story told how she had escaped. Still another, dated months later, told how the same woman had been run out of Dodge City after pretending to be an English princess and bilking four men out of almost two thousand dollars.

The woman's description matched Laura Quantrill to a tee.

The printer's devil piped up. "Here comes the owner, sir. You can ask him about rates and—"

"Got to be going. I'll see to my printing some other time." Slocum ducked back out the rear door in time to see Mayes entering the bank behind another man. From the set to Mayes's shoulders, it seemed that Charles Jefferson had preceded him and none too willingly.

Slocum's eyes rose from the alley door to a drainpipe and a window hung with decorated white lace curtains. For a conservative banker intent on maintaining a businesslike demeanor, this seemed out of place. Hurrying back to the bank, Slocum caught hold of the galvanized drainpipe and began shinnying up it. He reached out and caught the ledge of the window. The curtains were pulled, making everything in the room appear indistinct.

But he was able to see Charles Jefferson enter and stand just inside the door—and Laura Quantrill lie back on the bed dressed in little more than frilly undergarments. She beckoned seductively to Jefferson, and he went to her. They wasted no time getting down to serious lovemaking.

Slocum released his grip on the ledge and dropped heavily to the alley. He smiled crookedly, knowing now how Laura kept her financiers in line. If Jefferson had even a two-cent piece left after paying his bills, Laura would get it from him, just as she had kept Slocum hanging around with those same feminine wiles.

She was a confidence artist, but she knew a great deal about William Quantrill no one but a daughter would know. And Slocum had seen tens of thousands of dollars of loot being carted off after every mission of Quantrill's Raiders. It had to be somewhere, and Laura might just know where it was. Slocum decided he would stick around and see how the hand played out. It might be very lucrative—as well as very dangerous.

15

September 30, 1882

Slocum worked with the rest of the men in the cavern to get the armaments ready for the assault on Fort Kanses. But every time Slocum started for any other than the few crates he had been assigned, he found his way blocked by a sentry. He tried to judge which of the boxes were considered out of bounds and which weren't. The more he counted, the fewer he discovered containing rifles and ammo.

"What's in all those crates?" he asked Mayes just before they moved out for the attack on the cavalry outpost. Slocum pointed to a mountain of new boxes, arriving in a steady stream from outside. No one checked the contents. They simply unloaded the crates and stacked them.

"What's it say on the sides, Cap'n?" Mayes spat and pointed. "I make out the writing to say those are rifles. And that stack? Dangerous stuff. Boxes of dynamite and gunpowder. The ones right next to them are ammunition." Mayes looked curiously at Slocum, as if wondering why he had been unable to read the stenciled wooden sides.

"Why aren't we using any of that materiél?" Slocum watched three guards pacing back and forth along the walls, protecting the newly unloaded equipment.

"We got enough for the attack, that's why. We gotta

keep something in reserve. You know them bluecoats aren't gonna sit still and let us blow them out of the water. They'll be after us in a flash." With that, Joel Mayes swaggered off to lord it over a new batch of recruits.

Slocum identified more than a single stack of boxes being guarded closely.

"We're preparing quickly, John," came Laura's voice from behind him. "With the money Charles Jefferson gave me last week, we were able to complete payment on enough rifles to outfit the rest of our force."

"The rest?" This surprised Slocum. "There are others than those here in the cave?" Adding together the veterans from Quantrill's Raiders and the greenhorn recruits, Slocum made Laura's army out to be only a hundred men.

"Of course. The New South cannot possibly depend on only this handful of men, no matter how brave," she said smoothly. He watched her and saw the young girl selling fake gold mine deeds. How much of an accent had she put on to become an English princess when she had swindled others a few months later?

"Where are they? Will they join the assault on Fort Kanses?"

"You aren't sure of that move, are you, John? You ought to be. I have planned this carefully. We need to eliminate the outpost to insure our occupation of Kansas City goes without opposition."

Slocum had to laugh at that. "Every man in Kansas City will stick a six-shooter through a windowpane to potshot at us."

"You don't understand the extent of opposition to Union rule," she said earnestly. "They will welcome us, if the bluecoats don't prevent it. This isn't shooting from the hip, John. I've given it lots of thought. We can win. We *will* win!"

The clatter of caissons leaving the cavern drowned

out more of Laura's speech. The woman motioned to Slocum to mount and ride. He saw that Mayes and many others from Quantrill's Raiders also rode alongside. Mayes accepted him, even if the others didn't—quite.

Coming into the cool light of day convinced Slocum that fall was poking around and winter wouldn't be far off. Not the best time of year to start a war. With the Federals in control of the country, any abortive attack now let them take six or eight months to study the situation, assemble forces, and crush opposition come springtime. Even if Laura ordered guerrilla activity such as Quantrill's Raiders was famous for waging, they couldn't do enough damage to make the skirmish into a real war.

All they'd do would be irritate the sodbusters and others who had moved into this country. During the War Between the States, half the countryside had supported the South. Half had been related. Waves of immigration, westward movement, the coming of the rails, and the growth of mercantilism had done away with such support.

But Slocum wasn't about to argue with Laura over this. She had her own plans, and if he was clever and quick enough, he could cash in on them, too.

The band of eighty rattled and clanked across the prairie, dragging three cannons. Two freight wagons laden with spare arms followed, and the caissons behind the wagons. Slocum noted that Laura had overlooked the need for food and water. It was a hard day's ride to the small outpost, and Laura sent more than half her force ranging for game and anything they could beg, borrow, or steal from settlers along the road.

"They know we're coming," Slocum said. "They'd have to be deaf and blind not to."

"Of course they know we're going to attack," Laura said easily. "Since their pitiful attack on our hideout, they've known we would attack. That will make our victory, when it comes, all the sweeter. We will have shown those who are unsure of our power how strong we really are."

"Think you can get even more donations to the cause, then?" asked Slocum. He had poked around hunting for the map Laura claimed to have. She either had it too well hidden for him ever to find or the map didn't exist. He hoped that it did, that she really was William Quantrill's daughter, or had another source of information about the fabulous trove hidden since the war. Slocum could ride away a rich man if he got his hands on even a fraction of the money.

"Support will come from all quarters. I have been in touch with a group in Utah willing to support us, should we be successful today. And we will. We will." Laura Quantrill rode with her chin high and face catching the wind. In the distance rose the palisades of Fort Kanses. Her nostrils flared, as if she already scented victory on the zephyr blowing over the prairie.

"That's how you're deploying the cannons?" Slocum asked, startled at the pattern of the artillery pieces. It was as if the gun commanders had simply stopped and prepared to fire without any coordination with the rest of their troops.

"It will work, John. Trust us." Laura held her prancing stallion steady as she watched the gun crews work to ram in their loads.

"If you separated them, return fire wouldn't be able to take in all three cannons as easily," Slocum said. In the distance, he saw the sentries in front of the fort's gate scampering for cover. He worried that Fort Kanses had cannons of its own.

The cannons began spitting out their heavy balls. The first few rounds missed the fort entirely. Then one crashed into a wooden wall. A cheer went up along the front line of Laura's troopers.

"See? We can win."

"Win? You're just making them mad!" Slocum saw the gate swinging open and the soldiers wheeling out their own field piece. With military precision they began working to fire the cannon. When it belched fire and smoke, Slocum ducked involuntarily. The ball skittered along the ground and blew apart the centermost cannon.

The secondary explosion knocked Slocum from his horse.

"Run!" he shouted. "Run! The powder's going to blow!" The third explosion knocked him flat to the ground. He wasn't sure how many men were lost, but all three of the cannons were damaged. Laura Quantrill hadn't heeded his suggestion to separate them.

"Keep firin', boys. We got the bastards where we want 'em!" called Joel Mayes.

As if a miracle occurred, both surviving cannons fired. One sounded as if it let out a tiny gasp, then exploded, killing its crew. Something had plugged its barrel and the artillerists hadn't noticed. Whether by luck or skill, the third cannonball made a direct hit on the fort's field piece.

Fragments flew everywhere, killing dozens of the soldiers. Flames began nibbling at the palisades, then spread quickly. This was the sign for the guerrillas to attack. Whooping and hollering, they raced across the prairie toward the fort. As Quantrill's men had done decades earlier, these men overwhelmed their opposition through sheer firepower. Six-shooter after six-shooter emptied into the cavalry troop trying to mount an attack.

"We've won, John. See? It was possible."

Slocum stared in horror. Two of Laura's cannons had been completely destroyed, taking more than ten men along with them into oblivion. The third cannon canted precariously, a wheel shot off its carriage. Slocum realized that the cannons were old and unused for many years; Laura had bought them for a few hundred dollars each. Worse, the crews knew nothing of ballistics or the mechanics of war.

The veterans of her father's outfit came whooping and hollering back from their slaughter. Liddell rode up and saluted.

"We wiped 'em out to the last man," he reported proudly. "Weren't more'n a dozen of them inside."

"This is an outpost. The real force is at Fort Leavenworth," Slocum said. Laura ignored him, as did Liddell and the others. All they saw was complete victory. Slocum saw it as less, much less. This was a poke in the belly that would enrage the military commanders. They had the resources—the army—of an entire nation to draw on.

Laura Quantrill had to see that that might would be turned against her quickly.

"Back to the caves," she called. Liddell repeated the command and Mayes took it up. In ten minutes, the ragged column retraced the road to the limestone sanctuary. Slocum rode in silence, mulling over what had happened. Fort Kanses was a joke. It had been occupied by a handful of men, possibly the support company for the soldiers killed in their headlong attack against Laura's cavern fortress.

Any way he looked at it, Slocum reckoned they had less than a week before serious opposition formed.

"With this victory under our belts, men," Laura rattled on, "we can muster support far and wide. We've fought their best and won!"

A cheer went up. Slocum knew better than to believe that the soldiers at this insignificant outpost were a crack unit. They had met and defeated cooks and supply clerks, not trained cavalry troopers. Slocum found himself balancing greed, for the store of money William Quantrill had taken during the war, against his life.

Since ending the cattle drive as a hand for the Double

Ought ranch, Slocum had been in trouble of one kind or the other—all of it dangerous. He had nearly gotten his neck stretched twice, and falling in with the remnants of Quantrill's Raiders was hardly a better fate.

"We'll strengthen our position, fortify and get the cannons in position. When the cavalry comes for us, we'll cut them down just as we did before." Laura Quantrill's high-sounding plan had a dozen holes in it. Slocum didn't bother pointing out any of them to her or the men so blindly following the lovely enchantress. They wouldn't listen, and opposition now would only get him in a world a trouble.

"Where are you going, John?" she asked, as he veered slightly from the main track. He had thought to drift away, slip behind and then go due west. It had been too long since he'd seen Denver and the Front Range. Or the Pacific Ocean rolling through the Golden Gate. Fact was, Slocum would enjoy any sight that wasn't Kansas or Missouri right now.

"Horse is pulling up lame," he lied.

"Then get another." Laura ordered a half dozen men to stay with him. Slocum smiled crookedly and told her, "Must have been a stone under the shoe. Everything's better now." He tried twice more on the way back to the caves to work his way free, playing first on Mayes and then on two greenhorns. Whatever he did failed because of Laura's sharp attention and willingness to slow the entire retreat for him.

"Safety," Laura sighed, seeing the mouth of the cave. More businesslike, she ordered double sentries posted and the cannons swung about to cover the entrance. "We want to be ready for them, whenever they show up."

On into the bowels of the earth rode Slocum, cursing his bad luck. In the heat of battle had been the best time to slip away. The lure of easy money—and lots of it—had blinded him to a simple truth. Corpses didn't need money.

"Why so glum, John? You showed me you know your military tactics better than anyone else in our regiment."

He said nothing about Quantrill's Regiment and let Laura continue.

"Promoting you to colonel is the smartest move I've made in quite a spell," she said. "Let's celebrate your promotion. In my quarters."

Slocum wasn't about to turn down her invitation. As they went through the maze of rooms, he asked the woman, "Being colonel doesn't mean a whale of a lot, does it?"

"Why, John, what are you saying?"

"I won't be commanding the men in the field. You don't even trust me to examine the rifles."

"Check anything you like," she said, her tone changing slightly. She stiffened and slowed. He knew he had touched a sore spot with her. The coppery-haired woman hesitated, as if thinking hard, then spun around and smiled with all the allure of a courtesan. In a husky voice, she said, "Check everything, if you like."

Laura Quantrill moved so that her blouse came unbuttoned, just a little. Slocum got a view of the twin mounds of her breasts, poking up from her clothing like rising moons. His heart raced at the sight, and he knew he was being played for a sucker. He remembered the way she had lured Charles Jefferson to her bed back in Kansas City. She was spinning a web around him, too, guaranteeing his allegiance.

Slocum knew what she was doing and kissed her anyway. Their lips crushed together. Laura made tiny trapped animal noises and moved even closer, rubbing against him like a friendly feline. Her fingers worked to pull free the braces of guns stuck into his belt. Casually, she tossed them aside.

"Come on into my room," she urged. "It's so public out here."

"There's no one around," Slocum pointed out. His manhood strained painfully against his jeans. The way Laura's fingers brushed across his crotch, teasing and tormenting, drove him wild. He wanted her. He wanted her now.

"Inside," she said, tugging at him. As they went a few paces farther down the stony passage, Slocum saw a blanket hanging over a crevice. Laura spun around and vanished behind the dusty cloth door. Slocum followed quickly.

The room was subtly different from the previous time he had been here. The four-poster bed still dominated the room, but chests scattered around the room held Laura's clothing, packed and ready for travel. On the distant table lay a leather map case, a sheet of yellowed paper poking out from one edge. Slocum longed more to examine that piece of paper than to take what Laura so willingly offered.

But he didn't have a choice.

"Here, John, come here. To my bed. Take me now." She worked to quickly strip the trail-dusty clothing from her sleek limbs. Slocum tried not to stare at the map case but found his attention divided—until Laura reached out and pulled him toward her.

"What's wrong? Aren't I woman enough for you?"

"You're more than enough for any man," Slocum said. He grunted when she jerked open his buttoned fly and caught the long meaty shaft in her fingers. Laura began squeezing rhythmically, working at him as if she milked a cow. Slocum felt his balls tightening. He had to fight to keep control when she dropped to her knees and began lightly kissing and nipping at him.

He gasped as she took the purpled tip into her mouth and worked her pink tongue around and around. He was responding too fast; Laura Quantrill knew exactly the right things to do to arouse him totally.

"Get up," he ordered. Slocum reached down and

grabbed the woman under her arms. Lifting her bodily, he swung her around. She started to crawl onto the bed. He didn't let her. He pushed her forward, bending her at the waist over the end of the bed. Her buttocks shone whitely in the dim light.

Stroking over those taut ass cheeks, Slocum parted them slightly. He took a half step forward and found the target between her legs. He sank into her from behind. Laura arched her back and lifted partially off the bed. Supporting herself with her stiffened arms, she began rotating her behind in a small, slow twist that sparked Slocum's desires even more.

He was caught deep in her humid interior, her buttocks rubbed against his groin, and now she was torturing him delightfully with the movement of her captive hips. Holding on to her waist, Slocum let her move for a minute or longer.

Then he was no longer in control of his body. He pulled back, gathered strength, and slammed forward, the curve of her behind fitting perfectly into the circle of his loins. The power locked in his body unwound like a coiled spring. He drove back and forth with the power and speed of a piston, burning as he went. Laura's tightness contracted even more around him, making him think she was crushing him to death.

"Yes, oh, yes, yes, John," she moaned. She dropped facedown on the bed and rammed herself backward to meet his every thrust. This was more than Slocum could withstand. He grunted as he shot forth his load into her. Seconds after, he felt her body stiffen and begin to quake in response.

They both tumbled onto the bed and lay locked in each other's arms, saying nothing.

Laura finally broke the silence. "John, you're so different from the others who rode with my papa. You—"

Gunfire from the outer cavern interrupted her. Incoherent shouts echoed along limestone corridors and then came the deep-throated rumble of the cannons firing.

"The cavalry. They're attacking!" cried Slocum. He leapt from Laura's bed and hurriedly dressed. He worried that his last pleasant thought before the U.S. Cavalry killed him might be this lovemaking.

16

September 30, 1882

"Don't worry, John," Laura Quantrill said, lounging back on her fancy bed. "They can't reach us. Our defenses are superb."

"Our defenses are shit," he growled. He pulled on his boots, cursing himself for this dalliance. His eyes darted to the map case, then to the stone floor where Laura had dropped his gunbelt. He wished he had his Colt Navy, but it was somewhere else, probably in the Kansas City sheriff's office. The brace of six-shooters he had gotten from Mayes would have to do.

"Listen," she said, sitting up in the bed. "The cannons will cut them to bloody ribbons!"

"You blew apart a posse led by a town marshal and you destroyed an outpost, not a fort. These will be seasoned soldiers, not clerks and cooks." He settled his gunbelt and thrust four pistols into it. He still felt naked—naked and trapped like a rat.

"Am I really a colonel or were you just blowing smoke?" He settled the last of his clothing, wondering if anyone would notice or much care how he'd spent the last hour with Laura. She kept discipline using her wiles, and Slocum didn't kid himself that Laura Quantrill had somehow chosen only him among all the men in the cave for her lover.

"Of course you are. Why—"

He didn't listen to the rest of her fine speech. Slocum dashed into the rocky corridor and made his way to the large room. Smoke billowed back, blown into the cavern by a strong wind from outside. Every time the old cannons fired, more choking smoke made defense that much more difficult. Coughing, Slocum made his way across the cave floor to where barricades had been set up.

"We're blowin' 'em to hell and back," crowed Joel Mayes. "The damn fools rode smack dab into the cannon."

Slocum couldn't tell if Mayes's appraisal was right or if the former guerrilla was simply wishing for an easy victory. He saw the pieces of an army carbine a few yards away. A piece of metal had ripped it apart, and probably the soldier holding it.

"I'm going to scout," Slocum said. "Hold your fire for a few minutes, till I get back." Slocum waited to see if Mayes understood. The old blood lust was on the man. He wanted nothing more than to fire the cannon until its barrel melted. That would put more cannonballs through the front line of the cavalry troopers, but it wouldn't sate his need for personal slaughter.

"Go on, Slocum. I'll see to the crew. Get 'em some water, maybe."

"Good idea," Slocum said, ducking low and dodging through the barricades. He stumbled into one crate marked "RIFLES" on the side and was startled when he knocked it spinning. He dropped to one knee and tried to pry the lid off. It remained sealed, but Slocum knew there couldn't be anything in it or it wouldn't have moved so easily. He shoved his finger through a bullet hole and found only emptiness.

Shrugging it off, Slocum made his way out of the cave mouth until he reached a spot where the cool fall breeze carried off the cannon smoke. Settling down, he tried to figure out what had happened. He let out a low whistle when he saw how stupid the military commander had been.

Even facing a solitary cannon, an all-out charge was foolhardy. The officer must have forced his cavalry into a narrow mouth leading into the cavern. They were cut to ribbons, first by the cannons, then by the devastating fire from the stone fortifications along either wall. A quick count showed no fewer than twenty men dead or dying.

Slocum had started to move farther afield when a bullet took off his hat and sent it whirling through the air. He fell facedown and tried to find the marksman. Wherever the sniper hid, he was beyond the range of Slocum's six-shooters. Rolling to one side provoked a new round of fire that drove Slocum back into the cave.

"Open up on 'em again. Slocum's back," came Mayes's command. Slocum barely had time to clap his hands over his ears to dampen the cannonade.

"Stop, don't fire again," Slocum shouted. "There's nothing out there to hit. You've already destroyed half a company, maybe more." For all the bodies he had seen, Slocum knew there would be more beyond the cavern mouth. Comrades would rescue their wounded, and others would die more slowly away from the battlefield. He had seen only the ones blown apart by the cannonballs rattling down the narrow cleft.

"How many are left?" asked Mayes.

"I don't know, but we'll have to find out quick." Slocum brushed off his clothing, noticing he had lost more than his hat. Two of his four six-guns had fallen from his belt. He looked around and picked up others discarded by an artillerist. The man was intent on firing his field piece, not using the more accurate six-guns.

"What's the hurry, John?" came Laura Quantrill's soft voice. It cut through the hubbub like a knife. "We have scored a tremendous victory."

"Victory, hell," Slocum snapped. "They've got us

bottled up here. A sniper almost took my head off. With a handful of men, they can keep us trapped here until we die of old age. Where's your rebellion then?"

"John, John," she chided gently. "We're not trapped like rats. In fact, leave the defenses in Mayes's capable hands. Come with me. We have a mission to perform vital to the rebellion."

She took his arm and pulled him back into the cavern. Slocum followed, reflecting on how a woman as wily as Laura Quantrill would never trap herself in the caves. There had to be a way out.

"Get your horse," she said, choosing one for herself. Together they wended their way through tight passages that caused the horses to protest, but a steady wind blowing in his face told Slocum of another way into the caves—and a way out.

"We must go into Kansas City and meet with Charles Jefferson. He is becoming too insistent on certain . . . matters." Laura didn't have to tell Slocum what Jefferson's concern was. The rancher was strapped financially. He'd want results before he gave her a single dime. Slocum had overheard enough of Laura's conversation with the banker to know Jefferson had given her a bad check.

"What does Jefferson get out of this revolt?" he asked. Laura rattled on about freeing the oppressed and other irrelevant reasons, but as she talked, a clearer picture came to Slocum.

"He's bankrupt, isn't he? Charles Jefferson owes everyone and didn't get enough for his herd. He thinks a rebellion will change his fortunes. The son of a bitch."

"It seems Mr. Jefferson has problems controlling his own men. He had thought to enlist the aid of many of his cowboys for our cause. Not a one accepted his offer because he failed to back it up with gold or even green-backs." Laura mounted and rode slowly through a crevice into the afternoon sun. The light caught her hair and turned it into spun copper, the exact color hair Slocum remembered William Quantrill having. He thought it might have been coincidence, then Laura tossed her head and gestured for him to follow with a movement he remembered all too well as one of the guerrilla leader's gestures.

She might be a confidence artist, but she might also be Quantrill's daughter. Slocum couldn't decide. For the moment, he would ride with her and see where the trail led.

"There they are," Slocum said, pointing to a low rise. Atop it sat a half dozen troopers, their attention fixed on the mouth of the cavern in the other direction. "If we're quick about it, they won't see us."

"What if they do? We're simply riding on the prairie. We heard gunfire and nothing more." She laughed and urged her horse to a canter. Slocum spurred his gelding and followed.

"What do you want from Jefferson if he's bankrupt?" Slocum asked. "He can't help your coffers—your cause," he hastily amended.

"Charles Jefferson is a powerful man, rich or poor. In Texas his political influence could benefit our cause greatly. Oh, he has his uses, John." Laura fell silent, working over new schemes in her head. Slocum kept looking behind them, wondering if the cavalry would come tearing across the plains after them. Somehow they had ridden past the sentries and never attracted any unwanted attention.

Some people were good, some were lucky. Laura might be both. Slocum had learned not to bet against people like that.

Kansas City came into view a little before midnight. The lights made it gleam like precious jewels tossed out on a black velvet sheet. Not for the first time, Slocum considered getting the hell away from Laura and the city.

The sheriff still wanted him, and Slocum wasn't sure his luck matched Laura Quantrill's.

"Don't worry, John. The sheriff is out riding the circuit, serving process. That's the only way he gets any real money."

"You sent him out?"

"He's being paid a dollar a warrant, enough to keep him busy for the next few days. We have to decide what to do about the cavalry and how best to launch an occupation of Kansas City by then." No matter what the topic, she always returned to rebellion and taking the city by force of arms.

They rode to the back door of the bank. The outer door stood open a fraction. The heavier steel-lined inner door was secured. Slocum tethered their horses. By the time he joined Laura, the banker had opened the inner portal and ushered her into the small meeting room they had used before.

Slocum crowded in behind, seeing how cramped the space was. Four of Laura's financiers were in the room. That included Charles Jefferson, who stood in the far corner looking choleric.

"Gentlemen, the first shots have been fired—and we are the victors!"

"That's not what I heard," grumbled Jefferson. "You blew apart that old fort."

"Fort Kanses," Laura supplied easily.

"An outpost, really. And that drew the bluebellies to your hideout. They've got you trapped in there," Jefferson finished.

"Trapped? Colonel Slocum and I rode out with no trouble. They launched an easily repelled attack. Most of their force lies dead on the ground. We survived without a single casualty. Who is the victor and who is the loser, Mr. Jefferson?"

"They've sent for more troops. It'll take a few days to get them in, but they're coming from Fort Riley and

Fort Scott. You'll be facing a thousand soldiers before the end of October."

"We want to get this out of the way before winter comes, too," Laura said, as if the massive troop movement was part of her plan. "If these cavalry regiments were defeated, what then? Wouldn't Kansas be in our control?"

"Yes, but—" Jefferson sputtered. He regained his composure and said, "That's not going to happen. You don't have the men."

"We would be better off if you had delivered your promised company, true," Laura said, driving a verbal knife into him. "Even without these men, we can quickly recruit more. We have the arms, purchased with your generous contributions. All that we need are the soldiers for our cause. Money will buy them at first. Then others will rally to our banner!"

Slocum watched the reactions of the men around the table. For a group of successful businessmen, they readily swallowed her fine words hook, line, and sinker. It took Jefferson, who seemed backed into a corner both figuratively and literally, to ask the question the others must have considered.

"Where's the money coming from?" Jefferson coughed after speaking, looking at his cohorts.

"I will need more from each of you. As much as you can give, if I am to raise our army. We have a dedicated, veteran cadre from my father's former regiment. Men like Colonel Slocum will give us a disciplined officer corps." Laura gestured to where Slocum stood, arms crossed, in the doorway. "These veterans of Quantrill's Raiders can each command upwards of a hundred men— your money will let us bring an effective army of ten thousand men into the field within weeks!"

"In for a penny, in for a pound," muttered the banker. He shrugged and then said more loudly, "Count me in for another five thousand."

"Me, too." "And me." "Why not? We got to stop 'em soon or they'll take everything we own," came comments from the others. Only Charles Jefferson held back.

"We've been ponying up a peck of money," he said carefully. "It hasn't got us anywhere. You keep telling us about all the loot your father hid away. When you gonna dip into it?"

"Why, Mr. Jefferson, I thought that was clear. It is the money we use to *continue* the fight. If we squander it on the first battles, there won't be a cushion to fall back on later." Laura looked like an angel, but a hint of steel had come into her voice. "Are you doubting the gold exists?"

"Well, Miss Quantrill, I reckon I am."

Silence fell in the room. Slocum uncrossed his arms and placed his hands on the butts of two six-guns. Tension like this all too often blew off in violence. He wanted to be ready, if Jefferson went for the six-shooter at his hip.

Laura defused the bomb with a surprising statement. "Very well, sir. Let's go look at it."

"Now?" Charles Jefferson frowned in suspicion. "I'll want a man along with me."

"Just one—one you can trust," Laura said. "And Colonel Slocum will accompany me. Is that satisfactory?"

It was for Slocum. Nothing suited him more than getting a glimpse of the hoard laid away by William Quantrill. Slocum saw Jefferson's quick nod. Then the rancher said, "I'll be waiting outside for you."

"It won't take much longer here, I promise," Laura said. She quickly finished her discussion with the remaining men, then stopped the banker as he made his way out. Slocum overheard her whispered words.

"Be sure the money is in the bank. We'll need it all to purchase more arms."

"They're getting mighty expensive, Laura. I know an

arms dealer down in Indian Territory who can get us the same materiél at half the price."

"My supplier is reliable, Daniel. Be sure the money is here."

"It's all locked up in the vault right now, just waiting for the moment."

Laura grabbed Slocum's arm and guided him out of the bank. At the far end of the alley Jefferson and Horn Potter sat astride their horses. Slocum's finger tensed, then relaxed. He wanted a piece of Potter. If he took Jefferson with him getting it, that wouldn't worry him much.

"I have the map. Watch them carefully, especially when we get to the cache," Laura said. "I suspect duplicity. Be ready to use those six-guns. Am I making myself clear?"

"How bad you want his political clout down in Texas?" Slocum asked.

"Not that badly," Laura Quantrill said primly. She bustled off and climbed onto her horse. Slocum followed. Without a word to either him or Jefferson, Laura rode out of town, retracing the path they had used getting into Kansas City.

To Slocum's surprise she didn't head back toward the limestone cavern where the cavalry bottled up her men. She kept riding south, way south, until he wondered if she would ever stop. Once she drew out the map and made a big show of studying it, but she didn't let Slocum near enough to see it. Deciding on her course, she veered to the southeast. The rocky hills here promised more caves. Slocum wasn't too surprised when Laura suddenly reined back and pointed.

"There it is, Mr. Jefferson. Are you satisfied?"

"This is only a hole in the ground, Laura. I want to *see* the gold. Hell, woman, I want to *feel* it with my own fingers."

"Then go in and look to your heart's content, but

remember one thing. This money is on reserve for the New South. This will be the heart of our treasury, the soul of our new country."

Horn Potter laughed at this. Jefferson silenced him with a glance.

"I don't think it's such a good idea for both of them to go into the cave," Slocum said. "Let me stay here with Potter. You and Jefferson can check the stash by yourselves."

"A good idea, Colonel," Laura said. She glared at Jefferson, defying him to contradict her. Charles Jefferson shrugged and dismounted, handing the reins to Horn Potter. The Double Ought foreman took the reins and let his boss vanish into the black cave mouth.

Slocum dismounted and peered after Laura. A flare of light showed her lighting a kerosene lantern. Then even this flash had passed as she and Jefferson went deeper into the cave.

Turning to the foreman, Slocum said, "You've been stealing the cattle, Potter. Does Jefferson know?"

"What are you talking about?"

"You were too eager to frame me for the rustling. Wasn't Jefferson paying you enough that you had to steal from him, too?"

Horn Potter laughed harshly. "That old galoot is dead broke. He doesn't have two nickels left to rub together. I saw it coming, so I figured to get what I could on this trip. So what if I stole a few beeves?" He shoved his chin out truculently.

"You didn't have to put the blame on me. There were others rustling the cattle. You could have told the sheriff they were responsible—and they were." Slocum didn't bother telling Potter about Joel Mayes and the others working for Laura.

"Slocum, I never liked you. You was always too uppity. Too good to be with plain folks like me. I—"

A sharp report echoed from the mouth of the cave.

Horn Potter's hand flashed to the six-shooter at his side. Slocum beat him by a half second. Slocum's first two rounds ripped through the foreman's body before he cleared leather. His dying reflex blew the front from his holster, then Potter sank down, dead.

Slocum swung about, two pistols aiming at the cave opening. He wasn't sure what had happened inside, but he had to find out. Slocum hoped he wasn't walking into the muzzle of Charles Jefferson's six-gun.

17

·

October 1, 1882

Slocum pressed his shoulders against the cold limestone as he worked his way over the uneven ground to the narrow cavern mouth. Wind whistled through the opening, giving a mournful cry. Fetid odor told him of birds, and maybe bats, using this hole as a nest. Bending low, he duck-walked forward until he heard the telltale click of a hammer pulling back.

"Don't!" he warned. He had two six-shooters ready to spray lead out into the darkness. He couldn't see anyone, but he had ten rounds left. One, even a ricochet, would do the trick.

"Oh, John, it's you!" Laura Quantrill hurried forward into the dim light shed by the stars. She threw her arms around him and hugged him tightly. She had a derringer clutched in her right hand.

When Slocum tried to pull it from her fingers, she resisted and stepped away. Her head moved in a quick shake that warned him off. This was her gun, and the only way he would get it was from her dead fingers.

"What happened?"

"He . . . he did what I'd feared. When he saw all the money, he got greedy. He drew on me and I had to shoot him." Laura was breathless, but Slocum detected a coldness to her story, as if she had rehearsed it and only now got to tread the boards, to give her thespian rendition for his amusement.

But Slocum wasn't amused—or swallowing her story.

"I'll check him to be sure he's dead," Slocum said, pushing past Laura. He wanted to see the fabulous treasure left by her father. For a moment, Laura blocked his way, then she stepped away as if working on a new story.

It took Slocum only an instant to know Laura had lied. In the pale yellow light cast by the lantern he saw Charles Jefferson's body. The rancher's six-shooter was still in its holster. If he had gone for it as Laura claimed, it would have been out. Kneeling, Slocum saw the leather thong still looped over the hammer. He glanced up at her. Laura Quantrill stood silently, her face pale.

"The keeper's still over the hammer," Slocum said. "He didn't go for his gun." He reached down and took hold of Jefferson's wrist. Something was crumpled in his fist. Prying it loose was almost more of a chore than Slocum could handle. The dead man's grip was impossibly strong.

Though he had torn a corner off the greenback, enough was intact for Slocum to hold up to the light.

"That's part of my pa's hoard," Laura said, stepping up. Slocum saw that she still clenched her fist around the derringer. It had a single shot left. If she tried lifting her hand, Slocum would kill her.

"Are you a betting woman, Laura?" Slocum asked.

"What? Why do you ask?"

"It's a sucker bet telling me this is part of Quantrill's cache."

"But it's a greenback, a Federal bill he took—"

"The date on it is 1879. How'd a man dead for the fifteen years before this bill was even printed manage to steal it?" Slocum stood, wary of the woman. The cave was tiny, narrow, and long, going back into the ground. This small room, though, was packed with strongboxes.

Slocum flipped open the one at hand and saw stacks of new bills, maybe a thousand dollars' worth.

He turned slightly, the six-shooter in his left hand rising as Laura made a move to lift her derringer.

"John, you have it all wrong. I would never harm you! We're partners! We can come out of this the rulers of a new country!" He waited for her to put the derringer away in her clutch purse before responding.

"None of this is your pa's booty," Slocum stated. "You've been busy robbing everyone left and right. This is where all the money you've stolen ended up."

"Storage, John, it's just being stored. It's true this is the money from Jefferson and the other backers."

"It's more than that." Slocum leafed through the bills. There might be more than a thousand in this single box, and he counted no fewer than fifteen other iron strap–bound chests. "You've been sending Mayes and the others out to rustle cattle, rob banks, do a hundred small robberies."

"Yes, John, you're right. We needed more than those skinflints would ever fork over. This is the seed money needed."

"This is the money—" Slocum bit back what he had started to say. Laura had never intended for this money to be used for the rebellion. She had stolen it; she was going to keep it.

"There is another cavern with my father's plunder in it. Look!" She whipped out the yellowed map he had seen in her quarters. Laura didn't give him much chance to study it before tucking it away. "The other money is real, John. It *exists*."

"Why not show it to Jefferson?"

"He was greedy, a thief. If anything went wrong, I didn't want to lose the money necessary to finance the New South."

Slocum didn't bother pointing out the lies. If Jefferson had killed her, he would have gotten the map she had claimed was the only way to find William Quantrill's accumulation of spoils. This was quite a prize, this cave filled with strongboxes, but Slocum wanted more.

And he still wondered about Laura.

"John, it can all be ours—yours," she said, throwing her arms around his neck and kissing him hard. "Let's get back to the other cave. We've got to strike quickly or it will be too late."

Slocum didn't ask her what would be too late. He only nodded as she turned to lead him from the cave. He reached into the chest, grabbed a thick bundle of greenbacks, and stuffed it into his pocket as he left. It wasn't much, but he considered this a down payment on what he might win, if he played his cards right.

"Good," Laura said, snuffing out the lantern's wick. "I see you cut down his henchman."

"That was more a pleasure than a duty," Slocum said. Laura laughed delightedly and gave him another big kiss.

"You'll be my right-hand man, John. You won't stay a colonel long. You can be—"

"King?" he asked.

For a moment, Laura was taken aback. Then she recovered some of her aplomb and answered, "Even that, John, even that."

Slocum had a great deal to ponder as they rode back to the cavern, which was surrounded by cavalry troopers. Sneaking into the cave was no more difficult than getting out had been, much to Slocum's relief. He dismounted but did not lead his gelding back through the maze to the main room. He preferred to keep his horse here for a quick getaway.

By the time he reached the armory, Laura had already found Joel Mayes. She and the former guerrilla stood close, talking with animated gestures. Mayes seemed upset, but Laura calmed him.

And Slocum saw the way she stood on tiptoe to kiss

him. This was something more than using her wile to get what she wanted from a man.

Mayes slumped a little, then straightened as resolve flooded him. The pair talked for another minute before Mayes turned and strode off with grim determination. Laura turned her attention to the cannon sitting in the middle of the floor, being tended by its crew.

Slocum started after Mayes, wondering where he was going in such an all-fired hurry, but Laura saw him and called for him to join her.

"Where have you been, John? We need your expertise if we are going to break free. We need to mount our attack on Kansas City. If we want to hit before dawn, we can't take more than an hour routing those annoying soldiers." She gestured in the direction of the snipers still taking random shots at anything they thought moved in the narrow ravine leading to the cave mouth.

"Why bother getting rid of them?" Slocum scratched his chin. "All you want is to keep them away from Kansas City during the raid."

"Why, yes, but we don't want them coming up on us from behind. We might find ourselves fighting on two fronts, if resistance in Kansas City is heavier than anticipated." Laura eyed him suspiciously, as if he had tapped into her real plan. All Slocum wanted was to get a glimpse of the map she carried folded in her blouse. He remembered the path to the cave where she had stashed the booty from her robberies. He wanted more. He wanted all of William Quantrill's plunderage, too.

"Get the cannons firing to draw them," Slocum said. "They'll believe we're getting desperate and will try to escape. Make a feint while the rest of your force leaves through the back of the cave."

"That's a secret path," Laura said, frowning. She thought so hard, she began chewing on her knuckle. Slocum saw how she balanced the secret escape route against attacking Kansas City in force. He knew which would triumph, because he knew she wasn't committed to a New South.

All Laura Quantrill—or whatever her name might be—wanted was to pillage an entire town, one with its bank brimming full of greenbacks and gold from an active cattle trade.

"Very well. Fire the cannons, make a foray or two to draw the cavalry in, then we'll strike!" She spun and issued commands left and right. Slocum saw that many of the men, especially the newer recruits, were skeptical about taking orders from a woman. The veterans from Quantrill's Raiders snapped to obey, though, and this carried the rest along.

Nobody disagreed with the men who had ridden with Quantrill. The years had not mellowed them.

"Where's Mayes? He'd be perfect to lead the feint out of the cave," Slocum said. "I saw him do it when we rode with your pa." He knew Joel Mayes had left on some clandestine mission for Laura. Slocum wanted to see her response.

"He's scouting for us to be sure the way to Kansas City is clear," she said glibly. Slocum read the lie in her eyes and she knew it. A moment of anger flashed in those flinty blue eyes, then she settled down. "You muster the men for the feint, John. You're a colonel, after all. Earn your rank!"

Slocum nodded and went about getting a dozen riders to gallop out, whooping and hollering while the rest of the cavern's defenses fired as a cover. They lured enough of the cavalry out for the cannons to open up, and then Slocum had the riders dash forth again, as if trying to get away. He lost several to snipers, but the officer commanding the unit outside had to be certain now the men in the cavern were panicking. Slocum ordered a third foray, with a quick retreat.

"Keep doing it, the next expedition in an hour." He left a youngster, hardly eighteen, in command. Slocum knew he was dooming every one of the men to certain death. The cavalry wouldn't take prisoners, especially when they heard of Laura's raid on Kansas City. Still, some might be allowed to surrender. The old days of General Order Eighteen were past.

Working his way through the cavern, Slocum slowed and then stopped in front of a mountain of crates. With Laura and the others already gone, the sentries guarding the stash were tending to other duties. Slocum found a pry bar and levered one end off a crate.

"Rocks," he exclaimed. Slocum quickly pulled tops off a half dozen other boxes. All were filled with rocks or sand to give them weight. "I'll be switched. Jefferson and the others paid good money for boxes of rocks." Slocum knew some of the money in Laura's private accumulation came from money never spent on the armaments. He remembered the banker's insistence on getting lower prices for the arms, and Laura telling him she had a reliable supplier.

The supplier wasn't reliable—he was nonexistent. All she needed do was paint "RIFLES" on the sides of old crates and pocket hundreds of dollars. A few real shipments of arms was all it took to outfit the few hundred men she had under her command.

"A real sharp swindle," Slocum said aloud. He dropped the crowbar and rushed out of the cave, finding his way through the twisting maze to where he had tethered his gelding. He saw heavy tracks where wagons had pulled out of hiding and found other exits. Following one, Slocum soon overtook the wagon and its driver.

"What you have in the back?" Slocum called. The driver jumped, too intent on driving to notice anyone overtaking him.

"Got extra ammo for the occupation. Reckon it'll be needed for a few days till everyone comes around to acceptin' us," the man replied.

Slocum didn't bother checking the contents. It might

be dynamite and ammo, rifles, or maybe nothing much. Laura intended to hurrah the entire town and strip it of every nickel. That kind of banditry required heavy wagons to remove the loot.

Riding hell-bent for leather, Slocum sought to over-take Laura. He wanted the map from her before she got down to serious looting, but he arrived at the edge of Kansas City just as the first shots rang out. All around him came angry cries, and rifle and shotgun barrels started poking out of doors and windows. Slocum had no choice but to keep riding and try to find the woman now, and then get the hell out of Kansas City before the citizens understood what was happening and began shooting back.

18

Slocum tried to remember when he had felt more beaten and tired, and couldn't. Quantrill had pushed them to the limit. Dawn the day before, they had camped at the head of the Grand River, not far from the Kansas border. Slocum resented riding in formation, thinking it made them too vulnerable, even if it did keep the loosely disciplined men in formation and ready for battle.

"We're set to move, men," Bloody Bill Anderson said, moving back down the line of four abreast. Slocum nodded, distracted and weary. He had been expecting it. They weren't rested, they hadn't eaten in hours, and of course Quantrill wanted them to strike at the Union outpost near Aubry, in Johnson County, Kansas. Simply reaching the Federals would require another hard ride.

Someone near Slocum grumbled, and Bill Anderson swung about in a fury. "You, slacker! Are you turning yellow?" The man's handsome face contorted into a mask of utter hatred. Since hearing of his sister's death and his other family woes, Anderson had been completely out of control.

"Nope, not me, Cap'n," said the partisan. The guerrilla looked around, as if hunting for the coward Bill Anderson had singled out. "I'm ready to go kill me some Yankees."

Anderson growled like a rabid dog and rode on.

169

"Company, dress your ranks," ordered Slocum. "We've got some fighting to do before we rest." He rode along his company, making sure six-shooters were loaded and the men were in as good a frame of mind as possible.

"Cavalry, Captain Slocum, we got Federals comin' at us hard!" Slocum's scout came riding up in a cloud of dust, pointing over his shoulder.

"Ready!" Slocum bellowed.

At the edge of a forested area Slocum caught sight of Union blue. He shouted his order to charge. Better to catch the Federals as they filtered out of formation through the woods than to let them form for a proper cavalry charge.

A ragged barrage cut down two of the soldiers tentatively poking their heads from the woods. Then came a frightened shriek, and the Union cavalry turned tail and ran. Slocum halted him company short of the wooded area. He didn't know the terrain and wasn't going to ride full tilt into a trap.

A second scout came up, riding so fast he lost his black slouch hat. He didn't bother to fetch it, telling Slocum he had important news.

"Cap'n Slocum, you got 'em on the run. They saw you and hightailed it."

"The cavalry from Aubry?" asked Slocum.

"Captain Pike, commanding," the scout said, nodding in agreement as he caught his breath. "They must not have known we was so strong. There's only two companies of 'em, and are they runnin'!"

"Go tell Colonel Quantrill," ordered Slocum. "He'll want to know."

The scout trotted off in search of their commander. In less than fifteen minutes, the scout came back.

"Cap'n, the Colonel wants us to rest till nightfall. Then we're on our way north to Lawrence. I'm supposed to pass the word to the other companies."

Slocum waved the scout on. He was glad for the break. It took twenty minutes to get his men settled into a cold camp, tend their horses, and get started on catching up on sleep. But Slocum worried about this attack on Lawrence, Kansas. It had no military purpose. Quantrill—and Bloody Bill Anderson—wanted it solely as retaliation. Such missions could only inflame the civilian population against the Confederacy, no matter how much they might satisfy the guerrillas' need for revenge for the Kansas City tragedy.

Slocum drifted off, his hat pulled over his eyes. He came awake with a start, hands on his six-guns when he heard hard-pounding hoofbeats.

"We're movin' out right now," Bill Anderson shouted repeatedly. "We move out now, and keep it quiet. Slocum, get your ass over to the Colonel's bivouac." Anderson rode on, passing the orders.

Slocum heaved himself up and saddled his horse. In less than ten minutes he presented himself with Quantrill's other company commanders, the last to arrive. William Quantrill scowled at him for his tardiness, but Slocum felt no dereliction in his duty. He fought as well as anyone in Quantrill's Raiders.

"We'll be moving out soon, gentlemen," Quantrill said. He took off his hat with its gold cord and wiped sweat from his forehead. The August night was hot and close. Quantrill wore gray pants and highly polished cavalry boots. With his lavishly decorated butternut guerrilla shirt, he looked the world like a soldier, a fighter, a conqueror.

"We'll be travelin' silent, taking a few locals as guides. If we recognize any of them, kill them."

"What do you mean, Colonel?" asked Lieutenant George Todd. "If any of these folks are a'gin us, we kill 'em?"

"Yes," Quantrill said brusquely. "No prisoners, no chance of betrayal. We will strike Lawrence at dawn."

."That's mighty hard riding," Slocum pointed out. "We—"

"We will do it, Captain," Quantrill said coldly. "We are partisans, not some namby-pamby, hothouse flower unit. We travel farther and faster, fight harder and do more damage than any ten other cavalry elements in the entire Confederacy. And we're a damn sight tougher than *any* Yankee regiment!"

A cheer went up, and Slocum knew discussion of the merits of the attack had gone by the wayside. He listened with half an ear to the rest of the orders issued by William Quantrill, then went to ride into Lawrence.

"You say he just up and killed the farmer?" Slocum sat and stared at his scout.

"That's the way I seen it, Cap'n," the man said. "Lieutenant Todd claimed this fellow—"

"You said his name was Stone?"

"Yes, sir, Joseph Stone. The lieutenant claimed he was the fellow who had him arrested in Independence at the start of the war. He took a rifle and beat the bejesus out of him."

Slocum took a deep breath. The killing had started, and it wasn't the uniformed Yankee soldiers being slaughtered. Little more than a half hour until dawn and the real massacre. Slocum saw the way Bill Anderson whipped up a frenzy in his men. His wrath knew no bounds. Only revenge for his sisters burned in the man's heart. And in Quantrill burned something more, a greed Slocum had seen before. William Quantrill viewed this raid as revenge, a way of keeping his officers satisfied—and a way of drawing in more loot. The three empty freight wagons showed how much Quantrill figured to take in the next few hours.

"Final orders, final orders!" bellowed a courier. Slocum turned and rode to where Colonel Quantrill sat astride his horse, looking strangely composed in a sea of anger from his other officers.

"This is it, gentlemen," Quantrill said. "We divide into squads of forty-five. You know your targets. Do not fail me, do not fail the Confederacy!"

The rest of the briefing went quickly, and Slocum rode to his small company with the orders.

"You mind repeatin' that, Captain Slocum?" asked one guerrilla.

"The colonel said, 'kill every man big enough to carry a gun.' That's clear enough. No women are to be hurt. No children," Slocum said.

"How big's big?" the soldier asked. "If a li'l kid runs out with a shotgun, do we blow off his head?"

"Defend yourselves," Slocum said wearily. He saw Quantrill's signal for the attack. "Charge!" he yelled, joining the other squads of cavalry racing into the town from the southeast. Slocum's squad came in at Delaware and Adams, then split with the larger group of partisans at Quincy and Rhode Island streets. Quantrill's Raiders had the town of two thousand enveloped within minutes.

And then the killing started.

Slocum raced along, pistols out and looking for opposition. It didn't take long to see it. A man wearing an unbuttoned Union officer's jacket stood outside his house, a milking stool in his hand. He started for a rifle leaning against a barn wall. Slocum fired; so did a half dozen others with him. The lieutenant died under the barrage, and the partisans raced on.

"There, there's a whole passel of 'em," cried one of Slocum's sergeants. He and a half dozen others saw the recruiting camp for the Second Colored Regiment. Slocum lost count after eight soldiers died, pistoled to death before they could reach their own weapons. He raced on, leaving the slaughter of the other soldiers to his subordinates.

As he turned to ride along Massachusetts Street, he saw Quantrill and a few others in front of the Eldridge Hotel. Slocum felt heartsick when he saw what they did. They rousted the hotel's patrons, shooting the men and robbing every guest. The booty was tossed into the back of one freight wagon before Quantrill and the rest moved on.

Slocum heard Quantrill shout, "To the senator's house. We can get Jim Lane and hang the scoundrel!"

Slocum reined back and waited for his men to catch up with him. He motioned for his squad to follow Quantrill. Slocum caught up with the guerrilla leader as he came from Jim Lane's house.

"The coward's not here," complained Quantrill. He held a gold sword and waved a general's flag. "Boys, burn the damned craven's house to the ground. Burn the whole damned town to the ground!"

Bill Anderson whooped, let out a rebel yell, and tossed a torch into the senator's house. In minutes long yellow tongues of flame licked outward and caused the roof to collapse. But by this time, Quantrill, Anderson, and the rest were unleashing terror on the small Kansas town.

Slocum did his share of shooting, but took no part in killing the children. If a man shot at him, Slocum returned deadly fire. But he tried to keep his men from dragging men from their beds and murdering them in front of wives and children. He wasn't too successful. Blood lust had seized his company.

"After 'im, after 'im!" yelled one guerrilla. He chased down a man dressed only in a flowing nightgown, running after him as he would a frightened rabbit. The partisan gunned the man down, two bullets hitting the fleeing civilian in the middle of the back. The guerrilla let his horse trample the dead man before he turned to set fire to the man's house.

Slocum went through the fight—the massacre—in a daze. By the end of the first hour, many of the guerrillas had broken into saloons and were drunker than lords. By the end of the second, Quantrill was struggling to regroup his men.

"We've beat them, men, we've won!" Quantrill shouted. "Our scouts on Mount Oread tell us Federals are coming at us from the north and the west. Get the plunder loaded and head south!"

"South!" went up the cheer.

Slocum didn't immediately join the retreat. He dismounted and rushed into a burning building to pull out a hysterical woman.

"My furniture. I can't let it burn. My life's in there!" she sobbed, struggling to rush back into the flames.

"Your life's out here," Slocum said, dragging her away. She broke down, crying bitterly at the sight of her house going up in flames. Slocum turned and stared at Lawrence. Most of the town was ablaze. He had seen both newspapers burned out, but no women had been killed.

But he had seen young boys cut down, boys no older than eight or nine. Slocum mounted and rode from town, aware that some of Quantrill's Raiders still lingered. His face was blackened by smoke from the buildings, and his eyes burned from too much gunsmoke. He was exhausted in both body and soul.

Mostly in soul. Hundreds had been slaughtered in the attack, and to what purpose? Killing civilians did no good.

Slocum rode until he caught up with the main body of partisans as they fled back to Missouri. And then he pulled Quantrill to one side.

"A word with you, Colonel. It's important."

"Yes, Slocum, what is it?"

"Boys were murdered back there. Boys!" Slocum's rage grew. "Shooting a soldier in combat is one thing; we murdered men back there. And boys. I saw *boys* shot like they were animals."

"Captain, I must see to our retreat. Bill, tend to this soldier's complaint." William Quantrill swung his horse around and galloped off, leaving Slocum with Bill Anderson.

"I heard you mouthin' off, Slocum. I always knew you didn't have no stomach for what has to be done."

"There was no need for—"

Slocum never finished. Bloody Bill Anderson had two six-guns out and firing. The slugs hit Slocum in the belly. Burning pain exploded in his body and brain. He fell backward off his horse. He stared up at the hazy sky and watched the landscape wheel past.

Then John Slocum crashed to the ground, abandoned by his comrades, more dead than alive.

19

October 1, 1882

A bullet sang past Slocum's ear. Another creased his belly. He bent double over his gelding and galloped the tiring horse down a side street. Putting his hand to his stomach where he had been shot so many years before by Bill Anderson assured him the pain he felt there was old and remembered, nothing new and dangerous. Slocum straightened, but the twinge in his gut was more real to him than the lead still whining through the air. He had protested the way Quantrill had slaughtered innocents and had almost been killed because of it.

Slocum had spent months recuperating from those wounds. The flesh had healed, but the memory lingered—and it always would.

A whiff of gunsmoke made his eyes water. Laura's attack hadn't been as secret as she had hoped. The citizens of Kansas City, unlike those of Lawrence twenty years earlier, fought back. There would be no easy carnage today.

Settling himself in the saddle, assuring himself he hadn't been gut-shot again, Slocum rode on at a slower pace to rest his horse. He heard the woman's shrill voice above the sporadic gunfire and rode toward it.

"Blow it!" Laura Quantrill shrieked. A deep rumbling shook the ground. The side of the bank erupted in a shower of brick and dust. Three men made their way

177

through the destruction. Laura had chosen the spot to dynamite well. The blast had ruptured the bank's huge steel vault. The trio began dragging out strongboxes filled with gold and greenbacks.

Slocum had started across the street when a hail of bullets drove him for cover. He watched as the men, under Laura's guidance, emptied the bank and moved on to a nearby general store. They sacked only the most expensive goods. Slocum ducked again as a shotgun blast blew apart a rain barrel in front of him.

He chanced a quick look as Joel Mayes came riding up. The man hit the ground running and went to Laura's side. The veteran guerrilla spoke quickly to her. She kissed him, and Slocum knew there was far more between them than he had supposed. Even the way she had sent Mayes on his mission back in the limestone cavern hadn't shown this much passion. Laura hugged him close, then stepped back.

Slocum tried to figure out what she had said, but he couldn't. Mayes nodded and vaulted back into the saddle. Before he could put his spurs to his horse's flanks, a rifle shot rang out. The pitch sounded different from others. Slocum didn't know why. Then he remembered. It matched the one he thought had killed Mayes years ago.

This time there was no question of the man's death. Mayes flopped off his horse and lay in a heap in the middle of the street. He didn't move as Laura rushed to his side.

Slocum pulled down his Stetson and charged across the street, dodging bullets as he ran.

"Joel, Joel," moaned Laura, her face drawn with emotion. "You can't die. You can't!" She shook the man, but the flaccid muscles told Slocum Joel Mayes had finally come to the end he had almost met when riding with Quantrill's Raiders.

"Get out of the street," Slocum shouted. His belly ached as he thought of Mayes dying. He might fall next to the guerrilla if he stayed in the street. Slocum slid on his knees beside Laura and grabbed her shoulders. "Get under cover. Everybody's gunning for us!"

He looked around and saw that a few of Laura's men had fired buildings. Unlike in Lawrence, men came out, armed to the teeth, and formed well-protected bucket brigades to stop the fire before it spread. It seemed as if every window sprouted more barrels—and they were all aimed at them.

"John, I—"

The woman surged into his arms and sank down, a bloody spot forming on her chest. The ugly red spot between her perfect breasts spread rapidly, and with the departing blood went her life. Laura Quantrill had only minutes of life left.

"Laura, Laura," Slocum said, trying not to shake her. He wanted to rattle the truth from her lips before she died. Instead, he laid her across Joel Mayes's body. Her blue eyes fluttered open and a thin smile crossed her lips.

"John," she said, her voice barely a whisper.

"I've got to know, Laura. Are you really Quantrill's daughter?"

She smiled, started to speak, then died.

Slocum knew better than to mourn her passing, with bullets tearing at him. He reached into the bodice of her dress and pulled out the bloodstained map she had shown around as the route to William Quantrill's hoard. Slocum tucked it into his own pocket, ducked, and ran. A bullet tore off his boot heel, sending Slocum tumbling, but he came to his feet in the relative safety of the alley where he'd left his horse.

A quick look into the street showed the sheriff and a large posse moving to contain the men still trying to loot the stores. The wagon holding the take from the bank had overturned, the driver pinned under the wreckage. The invading force, so different from the one that had sacked Lawrence, Kansas, scattered.

Not a single guerrilla had lost his life in the Lawrence raid. Slocum guessed all would this time. The peaceable folks of Kansas City didn't cotton much to anyone coming into their fine municipality intent on thieving—and they had the hardware to back up their intentions.

Slocum vaulted into the saddle and skedaddled, trying not to draw any more gunfire as he left town. Not until he was a mile outside Kansas City did he slow, and then only to get his bearings. He touched the bloody map in his pocket and knew William Quantrill's cache was as safe as it could be. Laura's was another matter. She had added to it constantly, with the money stolen and swindled from her New South backers. Slocum headed for that cave, knowing a return to the main cave was worse than useless.

He had no reason to ride into a trap where the cavalry would capture him—and for what? All the booty in that cave had long since been removed, what there had been of it. Weary but driven by the need to get the hell out of Kansas with as much of Laura's hidden boodle as possible, he rode until he wobbled in the saddle.

A big grin crossed his lips when he came to the cavern where he had gunned down Horn Potter and Laura had shot Charles Jefferson. Wealth totaling thousands was soon to be his. Slocum dismounted and made his way down the winding path into the cave. He seized the fallen kerosene lantern and coaxed it to a fitful life. He frowned as he sloshed the kerosene around. He remembered more remaining in the lamp.

Going into the cave, Slocum's belly knotted up. All the strongboxes were gone.

"Damn you, Laura. You sent Mayes to move it all. You didn't trust me not to come back and steal it!" Slocum laughed harshly. Laura Quantrill had read him like a book. "But you didn't think I'd have this."

He pulled the map taken from the dying woman and spread it across his knee. Using the light from the lamp, he carefully traced out the landmarks.

Slocum spent a goodly time studying the map. It lacked certain details, but he thought he knew where the location of the cave holding the plunder from Quantrill's Raiders' years of scavenging—and Laura's newly acquired wealth. Tucking the map back into his pocket, Slocum left the cave.

As he returned to his horse, he saw the scuff marks on the stony ground, showing where Joel Mayes had dragged the heavy strongboxes from the cave. In his rush to wealth, Slocum had missed the obvious spoor earlier. He mounted, got his bearings again, and headed across the prairie, giving the old stronghold a wide berth.

In the distance he heard a cannonade. Slocum curved out even farther, not wanting any part of that fight. From the direction of Kansas City, he saw a few wispy columns of black smoke but not enough to show that Laura Quantrill's small army had much effect on the daily life. The only one to profit by her raid would be the town's undertakers.

And John Slocum.

As he rode, he wondered how he would cart off all the spoils. Quantrill had spent the entire war stashing money and goods. Laura had been at it only a few months, but the hundred or so dollars he taken earlier told of how effective her thievery had been. Slocum was going to be very, very rich.

Rubbing his belly, Slocum decided that it was his due. Bloody Bill Anderson had gunned him down and left him, the recovery had been arduous, and when he'd returned to Calhoun, Georgia, his family had died. A carpetbagger judge had tried to steal Slocum's Stand, and Slocum had been running ever since, having gunned down the judge and his henchman.

Slocum was due. He was owed.

The sun arched above him and then began sinking into the west by the time he reached the area where the map showed the treasure cave. Slocum eyed the ground carefully for any sign of wagon tracks. He found none.

The longer he rode, the more distracted he became. How could Joel Mayes have driven this far in a wagon and made it back to Kansas City in time for the raid? The man hadn't sprouted wings, yet the loot from the other cave had been moved.

Slocum almost whooped in glee when he saw two landmarks from the map. He pulled the yellowed sheet from his pocket, scraped off a bloody patch, and verified the hill and river combination. He rode down to the riverbank and watered his horse, anxious to continue. After the gelding had had its fill, Slocum made his way to the next landmark on the map.

"There, there it is. It's got to be," he said, seeing the telltale limestone formations that spoke of hidden caverns.

Even knowing he was in the right area, it took Slocum more than two hours to locate the opening to the cave. The sun had set, and every muscle in his body ached. But he pulled away the sage and other growth in the mouth of the cave with a passion belying his soreness. The scent of riches made his nostrils flare.

Slocum blundered into the cave, then pulled back when he realized he needed light. No convenient lantern would illuminate his way. He chafed as he took the time to make a torch of dried bushes, adding just enough greenery to keep the torch burning after the first rush of flame.

The smoke choked him, but Slocum hardly noticed as he made his way into the cave. For a few minutes, he worried he hadn't found the right cave. Then he whooped in glee. He knelt and picked up a rusted Colt similar to the one he had used during the war. It had been here for years, long, hard years.

Pushing through a narrowing in the passage, Slocum emerged in a broad cavern.

He wanted to cry out in joy. No words came. None seemed enough for the sight of hundreds of crates stacked as far as the light from his feeble torch showed. He rushed forward and swore.

"Rifles. Worthless, rusted rifles." He went to another row of crates, still expectant. Here he found containers of food long since rotted away. Rows of wood casks availed him even less. The whiskey in the poorly made barrels had drained years earlier as the wood staves dried and allowed leakage. But a final row of strongboxes made his heart leap.

Slocum rushed to the row of boxes. Each was secured with a rusted padlock. It took him only a few seconds to use the butt of a pistol to knock off the hasp of the top box.

"I'm rich!" Slocum cried, grabbing a handful of money. Then he stopped and stared at the money. He tossed it back into the box and rummaged through it. And the next box and the next, until he assured himself the strongboxes contained nothing but worthless Confederate scrip.

"So, Quantrill, you have the last laugh. Did you spend all your loot or was it really given to the Confederacy? Or is it somewhere else?" Slocum made new torches and made sure Laura's spoils weren't hidden somewhere in the cave.

He found nothing of value.

Slocum returned to the first strongbox he had opened and pulled out a stack of yellowed Confederate bank notes. From a packet of five-hundred-dollar bills, each bearing the pictures of Stonewall Jackson and George Washington, he peeled off a single bank note and tucked it into his pocket.

"To remember you all by," Slocum said. "Especially you, Laura." John Slocum made his way from the cave, saw that it was almost midnight, and decided to put a few more miles between him and the Kansas City sheriff. North was as good as any direction for a drifter and fugitive from the law. He located the Pole Star and began riding, memories and the five-hundred-dollar bill his only companions.

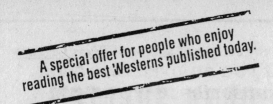

WESTERNS!

NO OBLIGATION

Mail the coupon below

To start your subscription and receive 2 FREE WESTERNS, fill out the coupon below and mail it today. We'll send your first shipment which includes 2 FREE BOOKS as soon as we receive it.

Mail To: **True Value Home Subscription Services, Inc. P.O. Box 5235
120 Brighton Road, Clifton, New Jersey 07015-5235**

YES! I want to start reviewing the very best Westerns being published today. Send me my first shipment of 6 Westerns for me to preview FREE for 10 days. If I decide to keep them, I'll pay for just 4 of the books at the low subscriber price of $2.75 each; a total $11.00 (a $21.00 value). Then each month I'll receive the 6 newest and best Westerns to preview Free for 10 days. If I'm not satisfied I may return them within 10 days and owe nothing. Otherwise I'll be billed at the special low subscriber rate of $2.75 each; a total of $16.50 (at least a $21.00 value) and save $4.50 off the publishers price. There are never any shipping, handling or other hidden charges. I understand I am under no obligation to purchase any number of books and I can cancel my subscription at any time, no questions asked. In any case the 2 FREE books are mine to keep.

Name _____

Street Address _____ Apt. No. _____

City _____ State _____ Zip Code _____

Telephone _____

Signature _____
(if under 18 parent or guardian must sign)

Terms and prices subject to change. Orders subject
to acceptance by True Value Home Subscription
Services, Inc.

14400-3